Peirene

GUÐMUNDUR ANDRI THORSSON

TRANSLATED FROM THE ICELANDIC
BY BJÖRG ÁRNADÓTTIR AND
ANDREW CAUTHERY

Valeyrarvalsinn

AUTHOR

Guðmundur Andri Thorsson was born in 1957 in Reykjavík. He works as a writer, translator, editor and newspaper columnist and has published ten books, including four novels. *And the Wind Sees All* was nominated for the Nordic Council Literature Prize 2012 and chosen as one of the fifty best books published in Denmark in 2014. It is the first of Thorsson's books to be translated into English.

TRANSLATORS

Andrew Cauthery read Law at Oxford. After graduation, he played oboe in the Iceland Symphony Orchestra (and learned Icelandic). Björg Árnadóttir completed a three-year course at the National Theatre of Iceland Drama School. She has worked as an actor in Iceland and England.

Together, they have translated English books into Icelandic, including *The Wind in the Willows* for Iceland State Radio and *A Map of Nowhere* by Gillian Cross, and Icelandic books into English, such as three crime novels by Victor Arnar Ingólfsson and *The Super Book of Science* by Vilhelm Anton Jónsson.

MEIKE ZIERVOGEL
PEIRENE PRESS

Reading this book was like embarking on a gentle journey – with music in my ears and wind in my hair. Yes, there is some darkness in the tales, and not every character is happy. But the story is told with such empathy that I couldn't help but smile and forgive the flaws that make us human.

First published in Great Britain in 2018 by
Peirene Press Ltd
17 Cheverton Road
London N19 3BB
www.peirenepress.com

First published under the original Icelandic language title *Valeyrarvalsinn*
Copyright © Guðmundur Andri Thorsson, 2011

Published by agreement with Forlagið, www.forlagid.is

This translation © Björg Árnadóttir and Andrew Cauthery, 2018

With special thanks to Gesche Ipsen, who edited *And the Wind Sees All* for Peirene.

ISBN 978-1-908670-46-5

Designed by Sacha Davison Lunt
Photographic Images: avesun / 123RF Stock Photo (polka dot dress);
Andrew Toscin / flickr / CC.4.0 (bike)
Typeset by Tetragon, London
Printed and bound by T J International, Padstow, Cornwall

This book has been translated with financial support from:

 **ICELANDIC LITERATURE CENTER**

Peirene

GUÐMUNDUR ANDRI THORSSON

TRANSLATED FROM THE ICELANDIC BY BJÖRG ÁRNADÓTTIR AND ANDREW CAUTHERY

And the Wind Sees All

In memory of my father
Thor Vilhjálmsson (1925–2011)

It Comes in off the Sea...

The mist. It comes in off the sea and slides along the spit. Every summer's day, it creeps up the fjord as evening approaches, noses around the slopes and foothills and slips into the village, where it curls around the boats in the harbour and licks the corners of the houses, before lifting itself just enough for me to be able to peep through people's windows.

I see the secrets. I see people cooking, peeing, pottering or skulking about. Some weep, some listen, some stare. I see people silent, or screaming into their pillows. I see people throwing out rubbish and useless memories, and I don't look away. I never look away. I see all.

Jósa is on her own, sipping lukewarm beer from a can as she scans her old school photos, to put them up on Facebook. Kalli is relaxing in the barn, following a wagtail with his eyes. Dr Jónas sits, head drooping. Lalli Puffin has gone for a walk and is about to bump into his sister, Lára, to whom he hasn't spoken for years and years... And here's Sveinsína, scratching herself between the shoulder blades with a wooden spoon; she is going to pop over to Jósa's to celebrate the day. But by then I will have vanished with the grey mist.

We creep on around the corner of a house. The mist hurries ahead of me as if it should be somewhere else by now, impatient with my loitering. Yet we both linger by the red house with the grey roof, where the children are getting over their colds and little Una has at last stopped crying. The secrets of a village – not all of them are important. Still, we peep through windows like an inquisitive god who wants to reassure himself that daily life continues to take its course, even though he has bestowed free will unto man.

The mist. It comes in off the sea and slides along the spit. Accompanied by a chill, and welcomed by nobody. Nonetheless, as we approach Smyrill the poet feels inspired. He stands up from his toils and takes out his battered brown notebook, goes into the kitchen and gazes through the window into the blue yonder. Then he scribbles down some ideas for his cycle of poems *Aroma of Ashes*.

The mist. It comes in off the sea and slides along the spit, and the villagers see in it everything that is grey – the cold silence that sometimes creeps into life here, just as it has now draped Svarri, the mountain that stands guard over everything. And then evening comes. And then night. And with night comes the rain.

Passions wake and flowers die. People lose heart halfway up the hill as headlights disappear into the blackness. A candle flickers in the breeze. Moments remain in the mind, while days pass, weeks pass, months pass. Seasons and years pass. I see the blue of the April sky and the green of the grass in May. I see the beating of wings as the south draws near, hear a new resonance in the swishing of the grass. I see the red in the children's cheeks in summer, after they've been outside playing all day. I see the autumn weather in closed faces. I sense the smell of winter, before death spreads across the land. Fuel pumps stand alone in snowdrifts. Boats creak against their moorings. The silence of the village during white, dark days. The silence of the mountain, the bleakness between the houses.

I have seen love awaken in a glance and die in deeds. I have seen an abandoned child stop crying. I have seen men drown and boys hang themselves. I have seen a pregnant woman with ice-blue eyes murdered and buried.

I too am long since dead. I should have been extinguished years back and perhaps have been, without having realized it yet. I am but a consciousness. I come in off the sea and slide along the spit, and soon I will have vanished with the mist. I am the afternoon breeze; I visit at around half past four and an hour later slip away to my dwelling, made of the past: of the grass that stirred a moment ago, the dandelion seeds that have floated to a new place, the folds of Kata's dress as she cycles down Strandgata on her way to the village hall.

The Clarinet and the Double Bass

The babble of children at play mingles with the afternoon sun. The air is heavy with the smell of food, the clattering of a motorboat out at sea is echoed by lawnmowers in the gardens. Shore birds hover silently, waders skitter about, dandelion seeds drift to the ground. The afternoon pulsates and gives her rhythm and momentum and hope as she pedals through the village. The houses are watching her, but that's all right. Old men with garden shears wave and call out 'Hello, Kata!', and that is good too. Children squeal and bounce on the trampolines that bulge next to every house, and shout 'Hello', and in the distance women kneel in flowerbeds and raise their soil-caked yellow gloves in greeting. Sidda, sitting in a group with Andrés and Fríða and others, also waves to her. And there's the man from the bass section, nicknamed Árni Going Places, standing on the steps of the old doctor's house with a pipe in his mouth and watching her. But he doesn't wave.

In two minutes she will be at the village hall. The Valeyri Choir is giving a concert tonight, an ambitious programme: they will be singing Icelandic choral songs such as 'Night' and 'Fair Little Friends' and favourites such as 'Be Ready When Springtime Calls' and the Swedish folk song 'Och jungfrun går i ringen', but also 'Locus iste' by Bruckner and 'Sicut locutus est' from Bach's *Magnificat*. Nothing must go wrong, it can't turn into a shambles.

All those endless Monday evening rehearsals where she has patiently sat at the piano going over the different parts again and again – repeated 'and again' in Icelandic so broken that you couldn't help but take notice of what she said. At times, with the Bach, it felt as if she was trying to juggle fifteen balls at once, and if one falls they all fall. At other times, it's been hard to get the fifteen balls in the air at all. There they've sat, these eager musicians, Valeyri villagers from the fish factory, the hairdresser's, the bank and the sea, from horse riding, unemployment and all the rest – each laden with a nickname and a history known to all, each labouring to synchronize their own *locu-hu-hu-hu-tu-hus* with all the others. But she has managed to get them to sing – loudly and firmly, and then ever so softly. She has felt that delicate sound between the palms of her hands. The Valeyri sound.

Now Kata plans to get there a bit early, before Sidda, Fríða and Anna arrive to set up the chairs. She wants to have a moment to herself, try out the piano, sit down somewhere, shut her eyes and feel a great, spacious C major chord resonate inside her. Then the others will come, smelling of horses and fish and earth and sun, weary from the day's labours. They will put on the gowns that Sidda has made and which will transform them into musicians. Then Kata will ask them to stand in a tight circle in the dark changing room, hold hands and hum 'Sleep, My Little Darling'. Afterwards they'll walk into the hall and arrange themselves on the platform the way they've practised. Kata will enter last, take a bow, turn to the choir, lift her hands and look into the eyes of each and every one of them. And then the choir will become one being. She'll give the signal and they'll begin to sing as one, create a new place: *Locus iste a Deo factus est...*

Everything is so bright. The evening is still to come and yet the day is gone. Existence pulsates at the edges. Kata is bare-legged and barefoot in her sandals, and she feels a little cool from the afternoon breeze that just passed by – not an uncomfortable coolness, rather an invigorating one, in the same way that the houses' eyes are not staring but encouraging. Everything is singing in the bright light. The sun sings, the sea, fish, telegraph poles, cows, flies, horses, dogs, the old red bicycle Kalli and Sidda gave her. She feels the day will come when her brown hair will once again have its red lustre. Once again her eyes will sparkle. Once again she'll sing inside herself as she plays the clarinet. Once again there will be life in her existence. Once again she will be loved.

She is wearing the white dress with blue polka dots she'd bought the day she was loved.

That day, she knew Andreas was going to propose to her in the evening, in the pavilion in the big park in the centre of Trnava. It's her best dress, the only one she will ever have. She hasn't taken it out since that evening. Carefully folded, it has waited inside her red suitcase in countless wardrobes for this June evening. It has accompanied her around the world on her travels through the labyrinths of purgatory. From her street in Trnava to Bratislava, to Prague, Cologne, Rotterdam, Moscow, Copenhagen, Hamburg and Reykjavík, it has stayed there in its patient folds, at the bottom of the red case beside her silent clarinet.

She would have been loved. After the rehearsal she was just going to slip back to her flat with her clarinet and change – put on the new dress – and Andreas was going to take his double bass home, and then they were going to meet at ten o'clock under the old poplar in the park, where they had always met after school, ever since they were youngsters: the clarinet and the double bass.

He would tell her that she gave meaning to his life. She would believe him. He would ask whether she felt ready to marry him and share her life with him. She would say yes, because she would believe him. And the evening would pass and the night, days and weeks, and within a few months they would be living together in the old town. He would play his double bass in the symphony orchestra and with the Trnava Stompers, the school jazz band they'd kept going, the old friends. She would play her clarinet in the orchestra and do a bit of teaching and would deliver mail in the mornings to supplement their income, as her mother had done before her. Days would pass, months. They would practise in separate rooms until lunchtime and then go out for a bite to eat because they couldn't be bothered to cook just yet – not until the children arrived, one, two, three. Days would pass, months and years. Little by little they would have fewer idle hours in which to dream; little by little their tiny flat would grow too small for them, sometimes food would be scarce and sometimes she would find it difficult to practise the clarinet in the mornings because of the children, but she would nevertheless press on, because her mother would help her with the children so that she could keep her job with the orchestra. Andreas would manage it as well, despite drinking too much and coming home tipsy in the evenings after having played with the Trnava Stompers in bars all over town. He would say that she gave meaning to his life. And she would believe him. Life was like that, after all – this is how his father had been and her father and their grandfathers, these men were like that. The years would pass, grey days, weary moments. They would argue because too much money was spent on beer, because the small flat was too cramped, because he did not pay enough attention to the children. But that was how it would be. It would work and she would believe him. She would still keep the red tinge in her brown hair that was reflected in the sparkle of her brown eyes, and her radiant smile that Andreas always said gave him strength to wake up in the mornings. And he would always look just as handsome in his red jumpers. Even if his belly got bigger with every beer-filled evening with the Trnava Stompers. They would sometimes be merry on Sundays, the whole family, while lunch was cooking on the stove and the vacuum cleaner danced through the rooms. And they would have their own private moments, the two of them, during quiet walks in the old park, where they always sat under the old poplar as they had done when they were youngsters, and as they would also have done that evening when he would have asked her to marry him, and where in the future, holding hands, they would have sometimes had a sandwich that he would have smothered in much too much butter, and a spicy sausage. He would tell her that she gave him the strength to wake up in the mornings and she would believe him. The clarinet and the double bass. She would have been loved.

After the rehearsal she was just going to slip back to her flat with her clarinet and change – put on the new dress – and Andreas was going to take his double bass home, and then they were going to meet at ten o'clock under the old poplar in the park, where they had always met after school, ever since they were youngsters.

The Valeyri Waltz

Last night, once the sun had set and the wind abated, and the eider ducks had tucked their beaks under their wings, while a lone seagull soared towards its cliff, and the timeless waves burbled on seaweed and stones, and seals yawned peacefully on reefs, and the people slept and there was no one about except him and the sheep and a few mice and perhaps a woman out on a farm who couldn't sleep, Smyrill the poet sensed how vast poetry is, how open the world, and how immeasurably far and high his own mind soared. He sensed restless creation within himself, the sky and the earth, the wind and the sun – the grace of it. He sensed, in the vaults of his mind, flickers of light come alive, flashing between eternities. He sat on a rock and with his eyes closed watched the pictures gliding across his mind. All kinds of people he had never seen and would never see, who had no meaning for him, slipped almost carelessly into his consciousness. He didn't know where they came from, whether they existed, whether they had existed; he let them slip away again, unattended, and brought his senses back to the night, the sky, the sea, the rippling grass, the swish of the breeze and the birds. He heard a resonance. He sat on a rock and watched the sandpipers scamper along the seashore like words dropped by God. His mind was immeasurable and for everything that existed at this moment there was a response. He could perceive all that was happening. In his mind everything became poetry: the gliding of the seagull a sonnet, the *pit-pat* of the ringed plover a quick, free verse, the rippling of grass falling dactyls, the maroon sky a hexameter. He heard a resonance. When the sun had set and the wind abated, Smyrill the poet heard and sensed that the poem was on its way to call on him. It came in from the sea and slid along the spit, it was the most beautiful poem he had ever written. It was about the shoots, the buds and the joy. It was about all that must be. It was about the tide on the shore, he felt it turning with the poem. It was about the gliding of the birds, the grasses of the earth and the gurgling of the waves. It was about the shape of the conch shells and God's living sleep. It was about the spirit that keeps vigil in the waves of the sea and makes the sandhopper hop, the bird soar and the bluebell droop. It was about the women who had touched him, softly and gently, with hands that cared and lips that opened and breasts that kept him warm during cold nights: it was about Unnur. It was about the power of grace. He heard a resonance. He worked quickly to carry the entire stream of his thoughts over into his little brown book, sensing and hearing that the poem was about to come to him – it would wing its way to him, the most beautiful poem he had ever written. He was both excited and calm, like an old hunter who knows that things can go either way but that the time for action is now. He sat on a rock and watched the sentences scamper along the shoreline, busily finding their place, trying to settle into the right molecular structure in order for a poem to emerge. He scribbled quickly. The words flowed from his pen, the letters forming pictures that did not look like the words they referred to and yet were. He wrote 'grass', he wrote 'sea', he wrote 'shore'. Writing these words, he created grass by a sea, on a shore. He wrote 'hands' and 'mine' and 'open'. He wrote 'bird'. He drew a bird. He watched the seagull glide about in the arc of a sonnet, the waves heavy with the ocean currents' thousand-year schemes, the clouds that on the deep-blue sky suggested white yearning. He watched the wind, watched the grass waving in the wind, saw the wind in the grass. He put the pen down for a moment, while he waited for the poem to come to him in its right form with the right words in the right structure. He began again to write, quickly and indistinctly, the words creeping forward like flightless birds tied to the book. He wrote 'her hair' and 'in a mountain cave alone' and 'in woods I watched at dead of night'. He wrote 'Unnur'. He wrote 'you' and 'from the south' and 'breathe' and then he wrote 'grass' and 'shore' and 'blue' and 'lands'. He wrote 'be you'. He sat for a long time, continued to write and look inside himself at people who floated there promising nothing, continued to look at the sea and the sky and at his own sense of loss. He thought about what had happened to him during his time, some of it beautiful, some of it ugly. He thought about the people with whom he had made, then lost, connection – the tender women, the good friends. He wrote 'grass' and 'shore' and 'sea' and these words described everything he had lost. The sea was deep, the shore was deserted, the grass was long. The sea was loss, the shore was loneliness, the grass was pain. The sea was cold, the shore was rocky, the grass was rooted. The sea was here and there, the shore was here but not there, the grass would not be here and never there. He heard a resonance. The tide had turned.

He stands at his desk in the kitchen, raises his pen and waits. In front of him lies a folder with his poetry cycle *Aroma of Ashes*, to which he wants to add a poem to read out at the concert later. He wants to read something new and he waits for it to come. When it arrives, it will feel at home. He has everything here. His books that cover every wall, including the basement's. His old harmonium, at which he used to compose when he was still doing that sort of thing – including 'The Valeyri Waltz', which continues to earn him royalties. The postcards he collects. The stones he brings back from the shore. His paints, pens, a pocket knife, some beautiful dead leaves. All his past shadows. He has turned into a barnacle here, as he'll tell anybody who asks why he doesn't move back south. Here he has his own life – and Unnur's too, even though she passed away long ago. When it flutters onto this white sheet of paper, the poem will feel at home.

He lifts his pen expectantly, takes a sip of cold coffee, puts his mug back down and looks up, stroking his beard. From the window he sees Kata Choir gliding past on her bike, her forehead wrinkled in concentration, wearing a white dress with blue polka dots. He smiles and scribbles something in the notebook lying next to the white sheet of paper. He writes 'sea', 'shore', 'grass'.

The poem has fluttered away into tomorrow, it has abandoned him. It has disappeared into the lands of limpid blue. He knew it had wings, sails, time, direction and tone. Everything flows. And tonight, when the sun has set and the wind abated, and the eider ducks have tucked their beaks under their wings, while a lone seagull soars towards its cliff like a sonnet, Smyrill the poet will return to the shore, sit on a rock with pen and notebook and wait patiently for his poem. He will hear a resonance. The song of the stars that sounds across the seven seas.

When I'm Sixty-Four

The afternoon teems with life. Standing on the steps outside his house after his daily nap, Árni puts his unlit pipe in his mouth and watches the dandelion seeds wafting in search of somewhere to take root. He hears the distant squeals of children playing on trampolines, the screeches of birds over the sea, the clattering of a motorboat returning to shore, lawnmowers, the burbling of a radio – and here comes Kata Choir on her bike, wearing a white dress with blue polka dots. He watches her pass and lifts his pipe, but she doesn't seem to notice him.

He goes back inside, pees, washes the slumber dreams from his face, brushes his teeth – taking his time, as if it were morning – and gazes into the mirror for a while without seeing himself or anyone else. He goes to his bedroom, feeling the old, worn wooden floor shift warmly under his bare feet, a welcome sensation – for a moment he feels his own childhood feet on this floor, when he stayed here with his grandparents. He digs out a stripy blue T-shirt and blue-patterned pyjama bottoms, thinking: *No reason I shouldn't wear these*.

He wanders into the kitchen, heats a pan of water on the stove and pours ground coffee into a filter, guessing the amount – although he knows it's right, down to the last grain. He takes the pan off the stove and tips water over the coffee, filling the kitchen with its aroma. He pours himself a cup, lifts it to his lips – but suddenly it's as if he can hear something; his eyes light up, he gets to his feet and goes back outside. He stands on the steps for a while, surveying the scene. He looks up at the church directly opposite his house, severe in its black wood panelling, he sees the mountain, feels the warm breeze on his cheeks, catches a glimpse of life in the village.

And goes back in, closing the door behind him.

He sits at the kitchen table and carefully takes a sip of his coffee, staring into the void in front of him. He doesn't listen to the radio or read the papers. He is swaddled in many layers of silence. He returns his pipe to its place in the rack that he'd brought down from the attic when he moved here. It holds four other pipes and he chooses a new one with the same care that he applied to sipping his coffee. He has a packet of Edgeworth tobacco that he has sent specially from England (using old connections). He keeps the tobacco in the fridge with a potato in the packet to stop it from drying out. He enjoys the fumbling around that goes with pipe smoking, and thinks: *No reason I shouldn't smoke.* He stuffs the pipe slowly – loosely at the bottom, tightly round the middle, loosely at the top. The *zip* as he strikes a match temporarily breaks the silence, and a moment later he is wreathed in the warm scent of tobacco and feels his mouth filling with its bittersweet taste. He watches the scented wisps of smoke wafting around the old timber-framed house.

Slowly he gets to his feet. Hanging on the back of his chair there's a blue cardigan, with brown elbow patches he sewed on one winter's evening last year; he puts it on, stretches and moves off to his study, pipe in mouth and hands in cardigan pockets.

When he came here two years ago, most of the villagers recognized him, wondered why he had come and concluded that he wanted to be alone. They all remembered his father, the world-famous champion trawlerman Tolli Tonne, for many years a Valeyri skipper before he moved south – cheated and moved south to become a herring king in west Reykjavík. Andrés from the museum said he remembered him as a boy visiting his grandparents in the old doctor's house every summer, but people still didn't understand why he'd bought the house – for a lot of money, as rumour had it, although the figures were somewhat fluid and became larger by the day as the story made its rounds. Most people thought that he was going to use it as a summer house, but autumn came and then winter and he was still there. He could sometimes be seen in a tracksuit, jogging around the village. Many found this strange, and Kalli said that he always ran as if he was on his way somewhere, so he promptly acquired the new name Árni Going Places and they stopped calling him Árni Moneybags, as before. Soon, he also started going to the swimming pool in the mornings and attending church on Sundays. Then, when the local choir's first rehearsal was held in the autumn, he showed up to sing bass. During the break, he talked to the others and happily answered their questions about anything and everything, and also asked them his own friendly questions. Regularly, at six o'clock sharp, he appeared at the Puffin, the little restaurant in the centre of the village, where he read the papers and chatted sociably with the manager, Fríða, and anyone else who happened to fall into conversation with him. He would sit for a while over a glass of wine before eating supper, which was almost always the same: a dish of cod with garlic, fennel and white wine that he had taught the chef – a former hairdresser and drunkard from down south in Hafnarfjörður – how to prepare; except on Thursdays, when he had a pasta dish with anchovies that he'd also taught the man to make. The odd thing was that he never actually seemed to go anywhere at all. He knew few people, despite having once worked a bit for Jói in the Valeyri Fish Factory; he occasionally visited Jói at home and played whist with him and his beautiful wife, the mayor and her husband, and old Lára, Lalli Lár's daughter, and other pillars of the community – but not Lalli Puffin, Lára's brother, because those two were not on speaking terms. He liked it here.

He conversed about fishing and the weather, the government and those in power, the president and bankers.

Occasionally he told stories from his former life. These weren't tales of fancy houses, silly money and conspicuous consumption – when asked, he said that he hadn't been part of all that financial debauchery, although he had of course known the principal players; instead, he sketched vignettes of meetings with the authorities, odd remarks in cloakrooms and embarrassing scenes at banquets.

He was impeccable. His demeanour was calm, his politeness unequivocal, his humility dignified. He sat in a corner of the Puffin, on an old family sofa that had once belonged to Lalli Lár, with his glass of white wine and an unlit pipe in the corner of his mouth which he would calmly relight from time to time – tall and slim, with a pianist's large hands that could comfortably span octaves, with blue eyes under half-closed lids. Sometimes he had a piece of paper in front of him or a paper napkin, and sketched boats and Mount Svarri – and Fríða. Sometimes, when she wasn't too busy, she would sit next to him, he being a man of the world and she having been brought up in Karfavogur in east Reykjavík, among poets and artists. She was of an uncertain age, well preserved, with hennaed hair and a beautiful body easily visible through her tight T-shirts and jeans, and sometimes he thought that she might visit him, breathless, late one evening, in the dark, to go with him to the old doctor's bed. He wasn't sure whether he would welcome her or turn her away.

As time went on others came to sit with him, and if someone plucked up the courage to ask why he had moved here, he replied that he wanted a break from people. 'There are such a lot of people down south,' he said, 'and they all want something from me... I wanted...' he said. 'I had to get away.' And he repeated it, dreamily and a little bit affectedly: 'to get away'.

The villagers sometimes mimicked him when he wasn't around: *to get away...* But they believed it. They never asked him for anything and never invited him to anything, but they were proud to be part of that distance he had sought. They felt the need to defend him and shield him from intruders, and when visitors arrived asking about his house and his circumstances they would close up and assume enigmatic expressions and say they didn't know anything about him and weren't interested in him, pointing at an abandoned house that had been empty for many years. Everybody knew that he had a secret. Everybody knew that he was guilty of something. Everybody knew that he was serving a sentence of some kind.

This morning he had come outside onto the steps as usual, freshly awake, and looked around with an expression of concentration, as if he had heard something. He had gone back in, drunk his morning coffee and lit his first pipe of the day, filling the old timber house with floating veils of smoke and a soft aroma, and then entered his study and switched on his computer. The day passed. He knew that although he was only sixty-four, he had, being on his own, become an old man. Here he inhabited a desert island. There was no one left. He would die alone among people who were, despite everything, strangers. He deserved this. He had not lived his life wisely. He had got carried away.

When he founded the advertising agency Tailwind in the mid-1980s, with Ágústa and a couple of their friends, it quickly became clear that he was blessed with a talent for life and work in Icelandic society. He was made for the job and the job was made for him. He was equally clever in every aspect of the business. He was a superb draughtsman, could compose a catchy jingle and a slick advertising slogan. He could bend words and make them dance in a wondrous way, sparkling in whichever direction he fancied; they would simply appear when he summoned them, hurry to meet his demands, obedient and humble. He did all the voice-overs for the television adverts himself, with a voice so full of yearning that everyone who heard it was struck by a longing for whatever it was promoting, and so trustworthy that they all knew that the surest way to satisfy this longing would be to obey the voice. His fleet fingers produced reams of drawings. In everything he did, his connection with the target audience's dreams and aspirations was so unexpected and clever that he seemed to be able to send people up any old blind alley in pursuit of the dancing words and the sensuous voice. His marketing plans withstood all fluctuations in consumer demand. He had a nose for business, spotted trends before others did – and the inevitable downturns too; he sensed the ripples in the nation's emotional life and knew when to provoke people into buying and when not to. He had a particular gift for picking up on those typical Icelandic crazes, which are like a prospector's seam of gold or a canny angler's bumper catch: skipping ropes, toffee, cars, shoes, coats, hair accessories... He became famous for casting his commercial net in waters nobody else thought would yield anything, but where he often reaped a rich reward. He was King of the Catch, just like his father before him – Tolli Tonne, who made his name in the herring years by going where his fairy godmother led him and landing tonnes of fish.

He knew how to read Icelandic society, he knew that it revolved around connections – making connections, being connected. Ever since primary school, he'd understood how to cultivate connections with everyone he met; everywhere he was the life and soul of the party, which was why his dentist was a personal friend, as were the builder and the Member of Parliament, the car mechanic and the bank manager, the bricklayer, the barber, the editor. Acquaintances old and new loved it when he sought their help and felt honoured when he asked them for a favour.

He read the times. The 1980s and 1990s were a period of revolution, when two conflicting economic movements met and would, sooner or later, end up fighting one another – and when that happened he would, if he was smart, be able to profit from the situation, be connected to all the individuals involved without attaching himself to either faction. He knew that he needed to have access to the old establishment – to the fourteen families that seemed to spread their tentacles everywhere, and were thus commonly called the 'octopus' – while still bonding with the new, aggressive killer whales, and even the squid, which most people underestimated but remained, nevertheless, a reliable source of revenue – yes, and the sardines and sea scorpions and cod and haddock and even the fucking sea urchins, he said with a grin one evening as they discussed things at his and Ágústa's home. And their two friends sat there, stolid and sociable, with no inkling that within a month they would be bought out of the firm.

There wasn't a living creature in the business ocean whose confidence and trust he did not enjoy. He worked for all political parties and all business sectors; he whisked up careers with a magician's skill. He created a sincere man of the people out of a recalcitrant dairy specialist; a sharp-as-a-needle, red-hot socialist out of a lifeless Danish teacher; a growling Reykjavík-hater out of a village idiot from the western fjords. He created people and trends, life and existence. With bold strokes and in unexpected new directions he shaped reality. He invented pop stars and fashion icons, brought bands together, and duets and trios. He would show up and say, 'No, you should try...' Or: 'Listen, have you thought of...?' Or: 'You are only supposed to...' Or: 'Remember...'

He sailed with the tailwind, controlling it for each and every customer.

He was always creating. Days passed – evenings, nights, months and years. He was happy. Sometimes he would glance at Ágústa in the evening, before he turned on his computer to continue creating, and think: *We should do something together*. She sat in the red chair in the corner of the dining room with her feet tucked under, reading novels. He gazed at the soft curve of her neck, her fingers fidgeting as she read, the blonde hair that rippled down her neck and that she sometimes twisted into all kinds of knots and ponytails and then released again to fall over her broad shoulders – there was an unrest about her, and he sometimes sensed this and thought: *We should do something together*.

But he said nothing. He disappeared into his computer and began to change the way the wind blew, for other people's benefit.

Sometimes he thought: *This is not life. This is just existence. We link our happiness too much to our success, we link our success too much to our well-being – and we link our well-being too much to our consumption. We link our lives too much to our existence.*

And yet he didn't know where such thoughts would lead him. To life? What was he to do? Try to make himself unhappy? Starve himself? Stop living in the beautiful house on Fjólugata, where thrushes and snow buntings sang in the garden in summer, and move to an old turf farmhouse? He mocked himself, thrust the thought away. But used it later in an advertisement for a new variety of tea.

They shared everything and took turns to do everything. He made his anchovy pasta and Indian dishes, poring over recipes and slavishly measuring level spoonfuls – as insecure in his cooking as he was self-confident in all his other creations. Ágústa, however, always cooked the same fish dish, which always tasted different – was never the same – always a new marine adventure. She constantly experimented with new spices and new vegetables and new shellfish, even if the basic dish was always cod and garlic, fennel and white wine. They drank a glass of white wine each as they ate; he loved watching the bracelets dangle from her wrists as she held her glass, waved it about and laughed with a kind of restless grace, as she told stories of her friend who kept walking into doors, or her mother, who was always begging her to give her a different hairdo but, when it came to the crunch, never dared to go through with it, or of eccentric cats she'd had, hopeless boyfriends, men harassing her when she was an air hostess, and beautiful paintings in cities around the world that had brought her to tears. After supper he chewed nicotine gum and drank a cup of coffee, and then moved into the old dining room, where his computer sat on the table that had belonged to his mother. When he looked up from his evening's work he would see Ágústa sitting in the red chair with her feet tucked under, cutting something out or watching television. She had brown eyes. He thought to himself: *We should do more together.*

*

On Thursday evenings they made love. He looked forward to it all week – perhaps this was a relic from when he was young and the television channels didn't broadcast on Thursdays. He would cook pasta with anchovies, which he found stimulating, and have it with white wine, which also stimulated him, and he dressed in an old red smock or a wide-necked tunic in which he imagined he looked attractive. Each time he touched her he felt a tingle. He touched her hair, cheek, neck, collarbones, arms, breasts, back; he slowly moved her thighs apart, opening her. She closed her eyes and opened her mouth, stretched, stroked his chest, grabbed the back of his head and pulled him towards her. The pleasure was overwhelming and fleeting. Afterwards, they lay naked, side by side, and talked about colours and poems. This was their open space. He lay on his back, with outstretched arms and an as yet uncomposed melody in his head.

They were a couple.

In the evenings they often sat together in the old dining room, he behind his big computer screen, she in the red chair, reading novels, cutting things out for her scrapbook, playing with her hair, lost in thought. An Arvo Pärt album in the background. Sometimes he went out and walked down to the town lake, even entered a bar where he would watch and listen to the girls – like buds of the coming zeitgeist – while pretending to listen to his old schoolmates trying to acquaint themselves with a new land-use plan for their over-mortgaged castles in the air. *Let's keep in touch*, was his usual farewell as he stood up and went out into the cool evening. Sometimes she would go out to meet her friends and sometimes she went up to the bedroom, dived under her duvet without a book and lay there, awake and open-eyed, looking into herself, closed. Her presence all the more tangible when she was not sitting in the red chair.

After three years together, they began to talk about maybe having a child. Three years later they began talking about maybe adopting a child. Sometimes she would phone her friends to talk about children, and they would all urge her to do it, quoting cases where it had been a great success, and sometimes she dialled the adoption agency's number as he sat with her, held her hand and nodded, but she always pressed the red button before the conversation could begin. Sometimes he asked, 'Shouldn't we get on with adopting a child?' At which she would nod, bite her lip and say yes. But the days passed, weeks, months, years, and she always pressed the red button before the conversation could begin. Sometimes she didn't go to work but lay in bed fully clothed under the duvet, her eyes open, looking inwards, closed. Sometimes she didn't come downstairs for supper on Thursday evenings, even though he had put on his red smock and had begun to cook his anchovy pasta. Then he ate alone and drank the whole bottle of white wine by himself, after which he went up to the bedroom and sat by her and stroked her head helplessly while listing ten points that made life worth living.

One evening she disappeared and didn't come home until the following day. He shouted at her, shook her, repeatedly slapped his forehead, but she remained silent and withdrawn, went up to the bedroom and climbed into bed fully clothed and pulled the duvet over her head and lay there, closed and open-eyed, looking into herself. When he asked later that evening where she'd been, she said that she'd been at a friend's place and had fallen asleep in front of the television. He knew she hadn't been drinking, but he didn't know whether she'd taken something. He knew nothing.

One Monday evening in autumn he was sitting at his computer, soft music coming from the record player – a suggestion of strings and densely woven low voices. She was sitting in the red chair, a novel in her lap. The room was cold. Outside, autumn winds raged, sending a chilly draught through the gaps in the ill-fitting windows. A curtain fluttered. She had a shawl wrapped around her and fiddled with its fringe as she read. Suddenly, she stood up and came over to him, distracting him from his screen. 'What are you doing?' she asked softly, and smiled. 'Am I disturbing you?' He shook his head but said nothing, smiled back. She stroked his head, and he felt a deep, strong yearning. He felt as if they were far inside a dark, ugly building with grotesquely winding passages, with ceilings so low that you had to bend down as you fumbled to find your way, and there was no music anywhere, just a low hissing, and no colours anywhere, just grey walls, dark walls. And all the rooms were the same. He felt

that they would never find a way out of these corridors
to the place where they should be, their place – the open
space after making love, when they lay side by side and
talked about colours and poems. He looked away from
the computer screen, turned around in his chair to face
her, took her hand, closed his eyes and forced a smile. He
couldn't find their space. He still felt that they were in a
cramped and dark place, full of hissing and labyrinthine
passages. And even though he had his eyes shut and a
smile on his lips that was supposed to indicate reconcili-
ation, and even though he felt this yearning surge inside
him, he sensed her fear. She hadn't touched him for a
long time and seemed unsure whether he wanted her
touch or was waiting for her to make her own way out
of this dark maze. He couldn't find the words to tell her
that her touch was exactly what he wanted. He stood
up, but he couldn't raise his arms. They hung by his side
like a puppet's; he couldn't embrace her. Her stroking
became confused, circling the same spot on the back of
his head, and finally stopped. She masked her insecurity
with a warm smile. He returned her smile, made a des-
perate attempt to find the way back to the space they
had shared before, by repeating some banter he'd heard
earlier in the day and found amusing. It wasn't the least
bit funny and her attempts to laugh both exhausted
and infuriated him. So now they stood there, the two of
them, facing each other in a hideous, low building in a
dark place, feeling nothing other than an overpowering
mutual longing. She was about to turn thirty, he in his

early forties. Her hair was blonde and shoulder-length, his streaked with grey. Both were tall and slim. Both had a dimple in one cheek. Both had long arms, long hands, long fingers. She had brown eyes, his were blue. Watching her move quietly into the kitchen to get some water, he felt that he had neither life nor existence. She went upstairs to the bedroom. He resolved not to sleep until he had found their space, retrieved her love. As he followed her up the stairs, he tried to compose in his head ten points that make life worth living.

When he entered the room, she was lying with her eyes closed and didn't respond to his attempts to wake her and tell her about the ten points. When he woke the next day, she was gone. She never returned.

First thing each morning, he goes outside to look around, then goes back in, goes to the loo, makes porridge, brews coffee, lights his pipe and returns to his study to continue writing his history of the village. He is always alone, every night all he embraces is absence. She went abroad, he thinks, somewhere south. To Morocco or Martinique – somewhere south, where the buildings are light and full of all kinds of arches and the morning breeze is gentle and people's skin is soft. The south would suit her well. She would be wearing a white robe, with long, grey-streaked hair, working in her restaurant, washing dishes, giving change, tanned and beautifully wrinkled, serving the families who would show up at six o'clock sharp to have a fish course that was still evolving but always based on cod and garlic, fennel and white wine. The sun would stream in through the west-facing doors. Suddenly she would think she'd heard something, her eyes would light up and she would go outside to look around.

The White and
Wonderful Dimension

The old couple sit at the kitchen table munching custard creams. Skipper Guðjón is thinking about the great northern diver he saw in the valley at Lake Valeyri yesterday evening, about its majestic glide along the lake and its long dive for fish, as if careless of time, as if free. Sveinsína is somewhere in the middle of Biggi's guitar solo at that gig in Austurbæjarbíó, the solo which, later that night, he said had been for her alone.

Guðjón drinks his coffee, the colour of a weeks-old puddle, from his special milk glass, the one he always uses. He slurps it through a mouthful of biscuit, enjoying the sensation as the dough softens and disintegrates, and the flavours of coffee and cream filling mingle. He is thinking about the great northern diver he saw last night, and the barnacle goose someone has told him about and which he has decided to look out for later this evening. His mind glides from bird to bird, as he gazes out of the window at the afternoon pulsating in the sunshine. He hears the redshank go *chew-chew-chew*, which makes him think of the oystercatcher going *cleep-cleep-cleep* as if wanting to hurry you along – he wonders whether they understand one another, the redshank and the oystercatcher. He has never wondered about it before, and yet he often thinks about birds and always watches them when he is ashore, or on holiday in the summer. The other day he spotted a little auk, and it felt as good as a big catch, being able to watch this tough little bird that had the sense to leave Iceland. Then he starts thinking about all the lads in his crew and their latest successful fishing trip, about the new boy, an undergraduate from down south, about Garðar the coxswain and his gallstones – he really should just get on with it and have them removed – about Teddi and whether he should be worrying about him.

Sveinsína takes a biscuit, decapitates it, then swallows it regretfully, half-chewed. Looking out of the kitchen window, she catches sight of Kata Choir cycling past. She is thinking about Biggi and his fair hair, always so clean and thick, and his guitar solo in Austurbæjarbíó, how it had seemed that it would never end, must never end, just got louder and louder, faster and faster, soaring further and further in more and more directions, louder, faster, longer. After the concert, everybody talked about his solo, how he had seemed to abandon his body and enter some *white and wonderful dimension*. It said exactly that in the *Thjóðviljinn* review published the following day: '…into some white and wonderful dimension'. She is thinking what a pity he never recorded it properly – never recorded anything at all properly, come to that, how nothing remains now of what he did or could do, how he'd never made much of anything, how nobody but she remembers him. She hears the solo in her head, enters it, stays there for a moment engulfed in the bright glow of its majestic chaos, soars...

She asks Guðjón if he would like more coffee.

'Ta, love.'

She half-fills his glass, fetches milk from the fridge and tops it up.

'Pastry?'

'Mm, please.'

She goes to a cupboard to fetch a bag of pastries and arranges them around the custard creams on the plate.

He says, 'Listen, Sveinsína. Teddi. I'm a bit worried about him. Maybe we should invite him and Gugga and the kids here for supper?'

'Sure. Give him a call. They can come tomorrow. He's singing tonight, of course, in the concert. Was it a good trip, by the way?'

'We caught a bit,' he says.

He is thinking about the great northern diver – its black head, its red eyes, its chequered back, how it glides haughtily across the lake, how it suddenly dives whenever it pleases and stays underwater as long as it pleases and catches whatever it pleases. He thinks: *I wish I knew what it's like to be free.*

She is thinking about that long winter when Biggi died. Teddi was only five years old at the time. They were living in a block of flats in Ljósheimar in Reykjavík and Biggi had started working in the Landssmiðjan metal works; at weekends he played at Hótel Borg with the Binni Frank Band, a bunch of old charlatans who played the notes mechanically off the page and never allowed him any proper solos – they wouldn't let him soar. She and Biggi had been just kids, really, and he was like a bird trapped in an oil slick.

'Penny for them?' he asks, dunking his pastry in the pale-brown coffee.

'I'm thinking about Biggi,' she says, stroking the handle of her cup. 'About that last winter of his.'

'Ah. Yes,' he says. 'Not much of a life.'

'No,' she sighs.

'Yes,' he replies.

'D'you really think Teddi is depressed?'

'I hope not. No, probably not. It's just a feeling. Silly of me. No, no. He's holding up.'

Their front door stands open. They can hear their family: Teddi and Gugga's kids squealing, the clattering of the motorboat *Teddi VA* as it approaches land, the distant din of the ocean that blends with the salty smell of the sea. They hear the redshank go *chew-chew-chew*, the faraway screech of the Arctic tern, the impatient oystercatcher's *cleep-cleep* demanding an end to all this feasting. Can they understand each other's twittering?

The sun streams in, fills every corner and illuminates their full, fleshy faces; thickset, broad-cheeked, eyes narrowed against the light, they are ox-sturdy and can lift anything, settle anything, deal with any problem.

'What about you, Guðjón, my love?' she asks warmly, putting her hand over his and squeezing it. 'What are you thinking about?'

'Nothing special, really,' he replies. 'How about we ride up the valley after the concert this evening? Look at the birds. You can take the piebald.'

'That'd be nice,' she says.

He is thinking about the great northern diver on Lake Valeyri and how it glided about in the pale summer night, filling the valley with its mournful wail – or was it laughter? Then suddenly dived, on impulse, just as if it knew how to be free, to be alone. She is thinking about Biggi and the long winter when he died, that winter in Reykjavík in that godforsaken block of flats, and Teddi was only five and followed his daddy out onto the balcony and watched him climb over the rail on the seventh floor and jump, watched his daddy briefly soar through the air – soar through his white and wonderful dimension – before hitting the pavement. He sometimes spoke about it when he was in his cups, said he remembered it, but she wasn't sure that was true. He says a lot of things, does Teddi.

One thing she does know: his spirit can soar, but also crash. He had been conceived in the rapture following the Austurbæjarbíó gig, when Biggi had played the guitar solo that went on and on, soared higher and higher, faster and faster, the solo everybody talked about – and which was for her. Every day she hears it. Every night, before she falls asleep, she sees Biggi on the stage in Austurbæjarbíó, wearing the purple shirt with frills, his full, long hair that was always so clean, and then she hears the music, bright and free, and it transports her into this white and wonderful dimension.

Evening Can Come

Life is outside. She sometimes hears it as it passes: there is a sound, a barely audible gust that she hears, and recognizes as life passing by. She hears children shouting and calling out, and sometimes she wants to open the door and offer them sweets or a Coke, but when it comes to it she loses her nerve. And they stay outside while she is here, inside. She hears planes and cars and motorbikes and lawnmowers and electric saws, and she thinks that this is what modern times are like. Everything moving so quickly. This impersonal noise. This loathsome brutishness. She is going to stay here, indoors.

In here. She has dusted everything and hoovered and washed the dishes. There's a leg of lamb in the oven, carefully seasoned with herbs from her garden: thyme, rosemary, basil and mint. She will feast on it when she has made the gravy and boiled a few potatoes, and it'll last her the whole week, maybe longer. The washing machine is purring away, and through the speakers Crosby, Stills, Nash & Young are singing dreamily about the fire and the flowers and the vase. She *la-la-la*s along in indistinct but perfect harmony. Everything is easy, they say. And now evening can come. The mist and the ill-will it had brought have disappeared. Evening light floods in through the window, unhurried and resolute in its thousand-year silence. The smell of lamb, herbs and cleanliness wafts through the house. She's had a shower and put on her neat grey trousers, and the blue T-shirt with the picture that her son, Gummi, had printed on it to publicize the place in Akureyri that he was running that year. Her hair is still wet and she has combed it straight back, making her delicate face look more rounded, with softly shaped cheekbones and blue eyes, a small chin and slender neck. She is young-looking, slim, with perfect manners in any company. Everybody warms to her. Somewhere she has old friends, and now she sits at the coffee table scanning old school photos to put up on Facebook, humming along to the music – Crosby, Stills, Nash, Young & Jósa. She looks up as if there was something to see outside the window, but there is only that foreign girl cycling past at the end of the road. The girl with the choir, which she would have joined if it wasn't for Kalli. She looks down at the faces in the photos, but sees only herself and Kalli. Later on tonight she might microwave some popcorn and drink a couple of beers as she watches television. Maybe an old film or a crime drama, or perhaps Benny Hinn on that Christian channel if he's on tonight. She finds him entertaining, though she isn't particularly religious. He's always full of life and fun; he reminds her of Kalli, with this boundless energy surrounding him. And he uses his energy to enter the lives of people who are going through a rough time, to fix things in an instant by shaking them up or getting the Holy Spirit to shake them up, she's not sure which. She herself has stopped bothering about cures or changes, because there's nothing wrong with her apart from life being outside and her not being particularly old yet.

She isn't old, but it's a long time since anybody has visited, a long time since she's met people, a long time since she has felt enthusiasm for something. Every day she goes to work at the bank, sits in her cashier's chair and deals with those customers who still don't bank online. But that's not the same as meeting people. On her way home she bumps into all sorts of people who say all sorts of things to her. But that's not the same as meeting people. Sometimes Kalli's sister, Sveinsína, drops by for a visit, sits at the kitchen table and talks about her Guðjón and her Teddi and other locals and their children and their in-laws and their in-laws' cousins and their children. But that's not the same as meeting people.

She is always alone. Occasionally Gummi rings. He came last summer, on his own. He'd asked whether he could come for the weekend, he wanted to cook cod for her and drink white wine with her, spend cosy time together. He is like that: considerate, sweet. And so he arrived just after noon on a Friday, his rucksack bursting with all kinds of spices and vegetables, garlic and ginger and coriander and dill, tomatoes, fennel and heaven knows what else, and bottles of white wine that he put straight into the fridge. He knocked up some dough for bread in no time at all, and was then off down to the harbour to see if he could get cod, but none was to be had so he went to the Bónus supermarket, where the only thing available was frozen haddock fillets. But he didn't lose heart. He went to see Kalli, his dad, in his barn, and then spoke to Teddi, who was up for going out with him to catch cod. That's what Gummi is like. He didn't stop until he'd managed to get the fish he was determined to cook for his mum. It was seven o'clock when he came back with two lovely cod, which he gutted and deboned. He opened a bottle of wine and began to cook while he told her all about what had happened in his life and she told him nothing about what hadn't happened in her life. This was a real moment. She listened to his voice that evening and watched the smile at the corners of his eyes and mouth. His words were scented. They were ripe with sweetness and exotic flavour, just as every bit of the cod was. His life had been full of energy and colour, and it had been happening outside while she was here, inside.

He told her for the first time about the restless years, when he was off in faraway lands, searching. His journey had taken him around South America and then Europe, where he ended up at the centre of the Balkan War. While bombs fell all around him, he had fallen in love with a girl with a long name he could never get the hang of so he just called her Ása. For an entire week they spent every moment together and in her arms he finally discovered himself. But then it was time to return home. They vowed that they would find each other when the war was over, and the last night she lay in his arms while the bombs fell outside, and then the morning arrived and the grey glimmer of daylight wreathed their existence with its reality.

'Didn't you know this, Mum?' he now asked, and she said no and stopped munching for a while.

'I still don't know what happened to Ása, just imagine that,' he said. 'She could be dead. I think about her every day, from the moment I wake up in the morning until I fall asleep in the evening.'

And once he was on night watch in a tent somewhere in Bolivia and suddenly he heard something. Maybe a rustle.

'Did I never tell you this, Mum?'

'No,' she says.

'Yes, there was this rustling, I thought I could hear something and then, suddenly, out of the blue, there is this guy on top of me and I feel – God's truth, Mum – I actually feel the cold blade of a knife at my throat. And I swear to God that to this day I don't know what happened, what came over me, where I got the strength from, but I yelled in Icelandic, "Get the fuck off me, you fucking arsehole!" or some such thing. And with this massive scream I somehow managed – with God's help or perhaps the Devil's – to throw the bastard off me and straddle him, and the next thing I know he's gone, and I'm left with the knife, screaming after him, "You fucking bastard!" or something like that. Did I never tell you this?'

No, he hadn't told her.

Then, in Ecuador, he'd seen something that he thought was probably a ghost, he'd felt the evil flowing from it. And there were girls – in Brazil, Venezuela and Mexico – but he loved none of them like he loved Ása in Sarajevo. He doesn't know what's become of her, but always dreams of looking for her and thinks about her every day.

He'd met the president of El Salvador and got him interested in Icelandic greenhouse production. He had escaped from ferocious apes in the forests of Brazil. He had paddled down the Amazon in a canoe. She looked at his receding hairline and his domed forehead, red with sunburn and hot thoughts, his once-blond hair that had acquired a strange yellow tinge, and his blue eyes flashing with adventure. She knew that he was lost, but perhaps not utterly doomed, since each mouthful of cod carried a new flavour as he regaled her eyes and ears with stories of his life.

He was forty-two now. She had been only eighteen when he was born. She'd sometimes wondered whether the fact that he was conceived in a church had affected his life. She and Kalli had been camping with other teen-agers from the village and they'd tried all night to make love, but Kalli hadn't managed to come because he was too drunk or something. She remembered how the rain had pounded the tent's orange fabric, how the whole night she'd dozed in a state of bliss, every now and again waking to a gentle orgasm, while he thrust away at her until it drooped, then started up once more when his need made him hard again. They woke around noon, got dressed and cooked oxtail soup on a Primus stove and drank lukewarm Coke; and then suddenly Kalli pointed at the church and said, 'Hey, Jósa, let's go and take a look at the church.' It was still raining as they left the shelter of the tent and ran towards the old, black country church. There was no sign of life from the other tents. The door squeaked as they opened it and sneaked in. They said nothing, didn't laugh or even whisper; it was as if everything fell silent when they entered. And it was brighter in there, as if they had stepped through a doorway into Paradise, where everything was sweet gentleness. They felt the angels' energy. The ceiling was blue, covered in gold stars. The pulpit was red and blue and green, decorated with crude paintings from Scripture. The altarpiece showed Christ feeding the multitude: he stood in the centre with outstretched arms, holding two small fish in one hand and five loaves of bread in the other, and around him were gathered a few men who were clearly local farmers intended to represent the multitude, though they didn't look particularly multitudinous. Jesus looked straight ahead, offering the loaves and fish also to anyone looking at the painting. Kalli and Jósa advanced slowly into the church. A red carpet covered the slightly creaky floor; the altar was bare, its sacred objects kept elsewhere. Kalli reached out and touched her. He stood behind her and ran his fingers down the small of her back to her bottom. She moved her legs apart. He kissed the nape of her neck, her earlobes, and stroked her bottom and crotch and thighs and back and breasts. She turned round and thrust her tongue into his mouth, and the Holy Spirit hovered over them as they took off their clothes, overwhelmed with desire, and felt their skin touching, warm and soft. And as he glided into her it was as if at last everything fell into place, and he came in less than a minute. For a while they stood like that, holding their breath, listening out for the Holy Spirit or perhaps the heavenly host. But all they could hear was the buzzing of the bluebottles on the windowsill, all they could see were the stars on the blue ceiling. And now they realized that they'd forgotten to shut the door behind them and it was wide open. A sheep stood in the doorway, observing them with disapproval, then turned and primly walked away. Giggling quietly, they hastily dressed, and they continued giggling all the way back to their tent. And all that week too, and afterwards, whenever they recalled their secret.

While Gummi was telling her of his adventures in faraway lands, his loves and sorrows, she wondered whether to say that she too had had her moments – rare and fleeting, admittedly, but they had nevertheless glowed while they lasted. But she kept silent. He also fell silent, while he carried the plates to the sink, rinsed them and loaded them into the dishwasher. He switched on the little espresso machine he had brought with him and made coffee, which he served with handmade foreign chocolates and apricot liqueur.

While they drank their coffee, he told her he was leaving Begga and the kids, that it was all over between them; he was going to come back to Valeyri and, to begin with at least, move in with her. He planned to buy the dilapidated old warehouse and open a restaurant there, buy a boat and catch cod, which he would cook for his customers in the evening. He was going to call the place the Three Cod. He sketched the logo he had designed, inspired by the flag of Jørgen the Dog-Days King: three stockfish on a blue background. She studied his forehead, his receding hairline and strange yellow hair, his eyes burning with absurd dreams. She sipped the sweet apricot liqueur and the strong coffee, and told him that he certainly knew how to cook cod, their meal delicious enough to be a national dish. She told him he was a good son, but that he must also be a good father and, more to the point, a good husband; if he was planning to come here and open a restaurant, which certainly sounded very exciting indeed, then Begga and the children must of course come too. He mustn't do as his father had done.

Life is outside. She sometimes hears it when she listens out for it – which she rarely does any more. She is going to put on some old records and have a celebratory beer while she scans school photos, to put them up on Facebook. She has checked her page once or twice today, and seen a few sixtieth-birthday greetings from former classmates. Sveinsína might ring. Gummi will definitely ring sometime later; he's like that, he will do that. He sometimes calls just for a chat and to let her hear his voice. She knows that he is hopeless and that the Three Cod exists only in his head, along with old stories – some true, some not – and his love for Ása, who keeps the Sarajevo locket he gave her to remind her of his eternal love and faithfulness, before he left her. He did leave Begga and the kids, just as his dad had abandoned his family when Gummi was only seven, leaving them with nothing but his absence. Now Gummi has a flat in the centre of the village and works as a cook at a nice restaurant nearby, but he still says he's miserable and he drinks too much. In a while she's going to make gravy to go with the leg of lamb, and after supper she'll have a couple more beers to celebrate the day, make popcorn and watch a film on television, maybe a detective film, or maybe just Benny Hinn, even though she's not particularly religious. And now evening can come.

Flying and Falling

There's always a certain calm as you return to harbour with everything shipshape, and all you have to do is aim for the beacon. Nothing else: if you stick to that, you're safe. If you forget to, you are lost, you end up in the shallows, you run aground. Simple, really. You go through the village and the beacon is your home. You go through your life and the eyes of the children are your harbour lights. The lights of hope are burning.

On *Teddi VA* all is shipshape. The lines are secured, hand reels rewound and fastened, buoys stacked and fish graded and crated on ice. A pretty good catch. And as you sit at the helm, steering towards the harbour, with this special smell in your nose, the comfortable sound of the engine in your ears, and with just the right kind of fatigue in your body after the work on board, and you see the afternoon chill with all its ghosts sneaking into the village – then you feel this calm descend, this special universal stillness. You know that, at this precise moment, Gugga is going outside to collect the washing from the line, wearing a white dress with blue dots,

Gugga with her chestnut hair, her broad shoulders that carry everything, her strong jaw and all-seeing eyes and now, yes, at this very moment, she glances across at the kids squealing on the trampoline, grinning over some nonsense you let slip the other day. Of course, she isn't actually wearing a polka-dot dress right now – what are you on about? – but this is the picture that comes to mind as you hold your course back into harbour, thinking all sorts about all sorts; as you think about your children, not in the usual terms of 'Come and eat your supper!', 'Put your sweater on!' – all that – but wondering what will become of them in a troubled world. You begin to think about yourself and what happened to you in the troubled world. And all that.

The boat slips slowly forward on the calm, cutting steadily through the water, a fulmar flying in attendance, satisfied and sated and on its own. Though you are always alone, you're never as alone as here. And when you are as alone as you are here – then you aren't, not really. When the universal stillness has touched you, you are alone with the sky and the sea, your catch, the resonance, the birds – and your beacon. There are laws at work in the world, and they are not the least bit mysterious or cold, and it takes no time to list them. Everything in life is simple; everything is very simple.

Such are your thoughts as you steer towards the village, drawing slowly and steadily nearer. And the village returns your gaze, observes your every movement, and yawns: *Ah, that Teddi*, it thinks absent-mindedly, maybe listening to the sound of the boat, and wonders if everything is exactly as it should be, speculates for a brief moment, casually, about your catch. *Ah yes, that Teddi with his usual two or three hundred kilos.* The village knows all about you, has seen the changes you have gone through, watched the greatest embarrassments at village-hall dances, seen the good, quiet moments too. Heard the yelling and the groaning. Remembers that yellow jacket you once had, and the red trousers, remembers your first drink, your first cigarette, your first kiss. And all that.

Right from the beginning you've sensed that the village is watching you, and forgets nothing. And even though you've tried to rise above this, to get away and live the life of a troubadour and sing songs about flying and falling, travelled all over the country with your guitar and amplifier and a lump of hash to get you flying, gone from bar to bar performing songs like the one about Old MacDonald and his farm and all that – even though you've grown your hair long and a beard and then shaved them, gained and then lost weight, taken to the bottle and dried out, found God and then hidden from him again – and all that – it's as if nothing can ever surprise the village; it's as if the village created you and knows what happens next. *Hey, Teddi, give us a song!* they sometimes yell, and then you do your best, although they know perfectly well what comes next; and that's what it will be like tonight at the party when you're done playing the old pop songs with the Óli Smarty-pants Dance Band.

The village remembers the album *Out of Your Skin*, which didn't sell. The village also remembers that review in *Morgunblaðið*, by some metropolitan smartarse pretending to be ever so fair but in fact saying: *Your life, your innermost thoughts – it's just crap, bugger off!*

The village remembers the wreck you were when you returned home with shattered dreams – and also that you heaved yourself out of bed, went back to the sea, behaved like a man, and soon had a three-tonne boat and a straight back. The village remembers everything.

As you head back to harbour you think: *You spend half your life trying to find out things the village already knows about you when you're born. However much you study yourself, your life and innermost thoughts, the village always knows a whole lot more. There are some women in the village who know Mum, remember Biggi and those bands he played in, know about Guðjón going south to fetch a woman and little Teddi after Biggi had flown from the block of flats in Ljósheimar and hit the pavement.*

That thud on the pavement and you're awake again. And begin to think about the washing on the line and Gugga, so big and strong, and the children bouncing on the trampoline, and you gliding back to harbour surrounded by the universal stillness. The sea gives sustenance and the companionship of birds, gives energy and nourishment for the brain. Gives the silence that is not silence but a kaleidoscope of sounds. Gives the peace that is not inactivity but motion. Gives the deep.

You fix your eyes on the beacon and begin to wonder whether the village, with the context it had prepared for you when you came here at the age of seven, really is the right place for you. You feel all kinds of currents in your head, deep undercurrents that might bring something new, were they allowed to mix with other currents. There is so much hidden inside you, in this depth. You're not even really sure that you're exactly the same as you were all those years ago – even though the village thinks you are; after all, the cells of your body are supposed to completely renew themselves every seven years. And, back then, there was so much that was bound to mess with you: the women, the pot, the drunken-troubadour life. And all that. And even if you have a little something tonight after the concert, there is no law that says you have to have another tomorrow. You are a father now and you own a boat, you have to measure up. Keep your eyes on the beacon.

Find your beacon for tonight's concert, so that you'll enjoy standing on that stage, even though Uncle Kalli will be singing his interminable solo – of course, the most important guy and all that, bless him. Gugga will be in the audience with the kids; you might even catch their eyes and wink. That'll be fun – that'll be a good moment. And then that party afterwards at Sidda and Kalli's, and someone shouts: *Hey, Teddi, give us a song!* And you take your guitar, strum the old C major a few times to warm up, and sing the song about the lights of hope that burn: *Hope restores your failing powers /*

Hope dispels unease / Hope soothes sleepless night-time hours / Hope's lights burn in peace...

There's this peace that hovers over you as you make for harbour. You are whole; you are complete. The clattering of the engine, the smell of oil and fish, everything shipshape, the fishy slime on your old woolly jumper, the fulmar flying in attendance, the boat's onward course, and your head alive with vague plans of which only the village knows. All this movement: the sea is eternal, it nourishes, heals, rinses, gives and takes, is made of currents that have been in motion for millions of years, slipping beneath each other in one continuous swirl, because the sea is, above all, movement. As you make for harbour, there is this peace inside you. The beacon is there, and all you need to do is to aim for the beacon, if you stick to that you're safe, whereas if you forget about it you are lost, you end up in the shallows, fall, sink into the deep.

Off Sick

Svenni lives in one of those houses that look like a man with his trousers hitched up far too high – a little house on big foundations.

He has been here for nigh on twenty years. He is industrious, resourceful, polite, but people find him taciturn and reserved. He has worked on shore for some time now. He's foreman in the refrigeration plant's machine room, and everybody who has dealings with him speaks well of him; he is kind and patient with the kids who work the machines, is fantastically hard-working and strong as an ox – a good bloke. When people encounter him at the swimming pool he returns their greetings amicably, with a big smile, but he never initiates conversation. Some were a bit surprised when he showed up to sing in the choir and proved to have a lovely tenor voice that added real colour to the overall sound. But he only turns up for the actual music-making, he doesn't take part in anything else. Everyone respects this. He envelops himself in a kind of cell that nobody dares breach, apart from old Grímur, his one-eyed, yellow-striped cat, and his sister, who lives down south in Sandgerði.

He called her up, just a moment ago.

Now he's sitting in the living room in his vest, talking to her, with Grímur snoring by his side. He didn't go to work this morning. He rang at nine o'clock and apologized for his absence, and he won't be at the concert later, not even after turning up to all the rehearsals and singing his *Sicut locutus est* perfectly. He is off sick.

He is always alone with old Grímur. He is always neat, he folds his clothes, washes them regularly, goes swimming every day, regularly changes the sand in the litter tray, feeds the cat at the same time as himself, does the dishes afterwards without fail. He does his own cooking, though recently he's been tempted to use the microwave more often than seems wise. In the evenings he reads old books on genealogy and folklore, and listens to the radio while playing patience. Admittedly, he never mows the lawn, so his odd-looking house is surrounded by long grass and weeds, and strangers might think that this was some sort of a drunkard's den. But far from it: inside everything is neat and tidy.

Not long before moving here, he'd met a woman from Dalvík and married her. They'd set up home down south in Hafnarfjörður, where he was working on the trawlers. Both did their utmost to make the marriage work, and perhaps it would have worked if they'd had children, but they weren't lucky. After living together for two years they both felt that they had no future. She finally moved back to Dalvík with another man, with whom she had three boys. He sent them Christmas presents when they were little – 'from Uncle Svenni' – but it's many years since he has heard from them.

He is off sick today. This happens a few times a year and, although he is sure that it's a secret, the village knows all about it. On these occasions he draws the curtains – an infallible sign – and digs out the bottles he's been hoarding for months, and stored here and there around the house as if hiding them from himself. He lines them up on the kitchen worktop along with some ginger ale and then begins to consume their contents with the same diligence and meticulousness he applies to everything else that he does, one after another.

He drinks only vodka and ginger ale, a sort of Moscow mule. He sits in his vest on the edge of the sofa in the living room, head drooping, his hands clasped together – apart from when he's swigging. Grímur lies asleep by his side in sympathy, trying now and then to purr, but he is so old that all you can hear is an occasional creak. In between drinks they eat prawn sandwiches, which Svenni has hoarded along with the drink. They have the radio on all the time to remind them of reality, but keep it turned down low. It usually takes him four or five days to do justice to all this, and after that two days to recover. When this is going on he always calls his sister.

When he was eleven years old he was sent off to the country. His parents thought that it would be much better for a boy to spend the summer months in the country-side than on the streets of Reykjavík, which would just mean hanging about like a slob and losing his appetite. He would become a pale, apathetic couch potato. In the country, he would find out what real life was all about. He would have to work like everybody else, he'd be outside in the fresh air, the breeze tickling his cheeks and making them ruddy and healthy. Working outdoors would give him an appetite and he'd learn to eat everything that was put in front of him. He would learn to speak the best proper Icelandic; he would get to know the animals, but more importantly himself; discover his own ingenuity when confronted with unfamiliar tasks, and feel his own strength as physical labour developed his muscles.

Sending him to stay with strangers was out of the question, so his mother spoke to her sister, who lived with her husband and three children on a well-established farm that wasn't too remote. They took him on a long, bumpy drive, and told him the names of all the mountains, rivers, farms and historic sites that they passed. 'See how beautiful and special your country is!' they said. When they reached their destination, his dad carried his green duffel bag for him and his mum patted his head as he solemnly shook hands with the whole family in the farmyard. They went into the kitchen and had coffee and doughnut twists. The three kids on the farm, two boys and a girl, were about his age; they stared at him, and when he smiled at them they didn't respond, but exchanged glances. On the radio an old man was listlessly reading the news. In the kitchen hung an unfamiliar smell of animal, food, sweat and earth. Maybe the smell of Iceland itself. The milk tasted strangely sweet, with an unpleasant skin, but the doughnut twists were soft and buttery, and there were some nice biscuits – 'Please, have some more,' said his Auntie Elín, while Uncle Jóhannes was cracking jokes. And there were also the old farmer and his wife, Jóhannes's parents, who made friendly conversation. They were all really nice people, but they didn't look at Svenni when they spoke, they looked at his mum and dad.

On the front step, Kátur the dog lay with his head on his paws, patiently waiting for the new boy to come outside and feed him biscuits. And when Svenni was allowed to leave the table and sneakily took with him a biscuit and a doughnut for the dog, Kátur pretended to be surprised, and showed his appreciation by placing his head on the boy's lap and letting himself be stroked. He was an old dog and a great judge of character. They sat together like that on the step while the adults finished their coffee and a discussion about the state of the nation. The breeze tickled the boy's cheeks and penetrated his clothes, making him shiver slightly. After a while, his parents came out, and he hugged them before they set off again, leaving him with these new people.

He learned to muck out the cowshed and to know each cow by name. He learned to drive the tractor and helped to move timber because farmer Jóhannes was building a new barn. He learned to herd the sheep, to shear them, learned to rake hay, to decipher the terse commands that were never explained, only repeated with the preface: *Come on, lad, didn't I just tell you to…* He learned knots and strange names for engine parts of cars and tractors. He learned new phrases and sayings. He learned to work and he learned to be silent.

The family were not unfriendly to him during those first weeks, but they didn't treat him like a child, more like an imperfect adult. The children rarely spoke to him; they went everywhere in a threesome, distant and superior like a secret order. Each morning he ate porridge mixed with skyr, which he hated with a vengeance. Maybe this was the real taste of rural life. He learned to switch off his taste buds and all his senses as he obediently spooned the colourless glob into his mouth and swallowed. He learned to eat food without tasting it, to be at the receiving end of meanness without getting upset, to listen to conversation without taking part.

The hardest thing was having to go out every morning straight after eating porridge and skyr to muck out the cowshed. The shovel was heavy, the stench was gross, and he was scared of the rats that the other kids told him lived in the cowshed. He sensed terror in its dark corners, thought he heard scratching and scraping, thought he could see them scuttling about. After a while he learned to be scared without letting fear control him.

The days passed, weeks, a month. Every day he helped with jobs around the farm; he often went to bed late with aches and pains in every joint and muscle, and the following morning he found it hard to get up to face the porridge and skyr and the cowshed. He learned to be tired but feel the exhaustion only physically. When he had time off, he would sometimes get a book from the well-stocked library and read about clairvoyants and interpreters of dreams, shrewd sheep and haunted cowsheds; sometimes he lay down in the heather by a brook and inhaled the scent of the earth and listened to the water's flow, and Kátur would come to him and put his head in his lap, have a biscuit and let himself be stroked. He learned to miss his mum without letting it get the better of him.

Sometimes, in the kitchen, with a bored voice on the radio reading the news in the background, his Auntie Elín would give him a hug, scratch his head and say, 'And how are you, young man?' And he would say, 'Fine,' gloomy but content. The Secret Three began to pay him a bit more attention, asking him about life in Reykjavík, telling him about all the various dogs that had worked on the farm – none of whom was a patch on Kátur – and also about shrewd sheep, lively horses, haunted cowsheds, strange men, and all the fantastical things that had happened among the hollows and hillocks that surrounded them. Rural life came to him without his noticing it, slowly and smoothly like the current in the brook by whose banks he sometimes lay with the dog. The old woman, farmer Jóhannes's mother, took him with her up the mountain, where she showed him herbs and explained how they worked, which ones tasted good together, and then invited him into the kitchen to boil them up, so that in the evening he was able to proudly offer everybody wild thyme tea. After lunch he was allowed to creep into the old farmer's room for a snooze at his feet, while the old man soothingly stroked his back and read him stories from the Sunday paper.

Days passed, hot and long, dense and wet, long-winded, abrupt, colourful, resonant, hazy, sunny. They began to make sense. He woke each morning with the usual list of jobs to do: the sheep, which turned out to be not at all smart, to be chased out of the field; the cows, which grew increasingly smart the more he talked to them, to be herded; the haymaking, the silence, the breeze and the toil. With each passing day, the shovel in the cowshed became more manageable, the rats in the dark corners more harmless, the cowshed ghosts more withdrawn. The Secret Three invited him to ride with them on top of the hay cart when they returned from the meadows, and they lay in the hay, giggling.

The owner of the neighbouring farmhouse would often pop over after supper to play cards or just to chat, while the evening story burbled away softly on the radio. He had once been the local MP, an important man, who still spent part of his summers here even though he'd long since stopped farming and moved south to join the rest of his family. He was a frequent visitor, perhaps because there wasn't much left for him to do out here in the sticks and he was bored. He was full of energy and humour, and everyone automatically started smiling when he came, because he knew many amusing tales about eccentric priests, malignant ghosts and clever farm animals. Sometimes his wife came with him. Then she would sit with her knitting in her lap, smiling faintly but perhaps a little smugly as he regaled them with stories she'd heard before.

Towards the end of the summer there was a harvest festival. The grown-ups drank vodka and ginger ale before and during supper, and became very jolly. They told Svenni there would be a dance later. Binni Frank's band from Reykjavík would be playing and they would all go dancing – he should come too, hadn't he brought his Sunday best with him? The ex-MP waved at him and said, 'Hey, come and sit by me, son! You're Pétur Ólafsson's boy, aren't you? I remember your grandfather very well…'

He launched into an anecdote about Svenni's grand-father meeting some strange man who said something strange to him. Svenni didn't understand the joke, but nevertheless he was proud that there was a story about his grandfather. The ex-MP told Svenni that he'd heard how hard-working he'd been and how well he'd done this summer. He talked with cheerful abandon about MPs and other important people – ministers, professors, priests, actors and radio celebrities – told stories of drinking, womanizing and witty comebacks.

At first, when the ex-MP put his hand on his thigh and squeezed it, Svenni thought that he must have suffered some kind of involuntary tremor at the dinner table which the man was trying to stop. Or that it was the man who was feeling shaky and needed to steady himself. The boy said nothing. The hand remained on his thigh while the man continued merrily slurping his meat broth with his spoon in the other. The hand moved further up. Svenni didn't know what to do to get rid of it, whether he should move away. He couldn't swallow any more. He just sat there, alone and helpless, while this paw continued its journey up his thigh, finally coming to rest between his legs, in his crotch. He knew that he should stand up, but he just sat still. He was only eleven and hadn't yet learned to stand up for himself.

He is off sick today. He has called his sister, to whom he doesn't often talk, being naturally reticent. He is on his second bottle of vodka. He sits in the living room in his vest, fidgeting on the edge of the sofa, phone in one hand and glass in the other. He is talkative. He speaks softly and his voice is clear – it's actually not that noticeable that he's drinking, he doesn't slur his words, doesn't repeat himself, doesn't ramble. But he doesn't stop talking. He talks incessantly. He talks about all sorts of distant relatives, many generations back, about whom he knows a surprising amount, and artfully traces their connections to each other. He laughs. He asks about her circumstances and her family, how everybody is and how they're getting on with what they're doing – which he's remembered incredibly well – with hardly a pause for her response, as if afraid that she'll slip away from his reach. And then

he begins to talk about the time he was sent to spend a
summer in the country at the age of eleven, and learned
to work and learned to keep quiet, learned to be tired
without feeling it other than physically, learned to eat the
food without tasting it, learned to swallow obediently.

'Yes, Svenni love,' she says quietly. 'I know.'

He doesn't raise his voice, appears far away, as if it had
nothing to do with him, as he tells her how the ex-MP
came into his room that night, woke him and led him out
to the cowshed. He describes everything he was made to
do and how he had to do it time and again during the
weeks that remained of his stay there, how he couldn't
tell anyone, how he learned not to feel anything.

'Yes, Svenni love. I know.'

Finally he falls silent, breathing heavily but otherwise
making no sound. At the other end of the line, she too
is silent. At last he heaves a sigh, drains his glass and
plonks it on the table. Grímur gets to his feet, hopefully
sniffs at the plastic wrapper of a prawn sandwich, yawns,
stretches, turns around a few times and then fondly prods
at his companion's thigh, looks at him searchingly with
his one eye and snuggles up to him again, creaking.

The Universal Stillness

Leaning back in his chair, Kalli rests his gaze on the centre of the doorway to the barn, which is standing open to the summer, letting in the generous rays of the afternoon sun. His breathing is light and regular, his diaphragm and soul in harmony. He is alone. He is at peace with himself, tranquil. And when, like black specks, bothersome thoughts appear, he waves them away. He finds this very easy, because he is, on the whole, quite fond of himself and indeed of all men. Just remember to breathe correctly, be at peace with your diaphragm and your soul, don't think about anything, not even about not thinking about not thinking about anything. His mind becomes light and clear and clean, and then maybe a thought will float in on a gentle sky-blue, a thought one may enjoy: a feeling, a memory of a feeling, a memory of an object, a memory of a feeling triggered by an object. Perhaps a memory of that splendid car he once saw, sized up, wanted to own because he felt that it was the ideal car for him. Perhaps a memory of last year's midwinter feast, when they persuaded him to imitate old car horns and tractors from the area ('*I* know – that's that old **Farmall from** Ásgeirsstaðir!') and people laughed cheerfully because they were happy. Maybe the memory of a blissful feeling he once had, when he was swimming in the rain and maybe after half a kilometre he had stopped thinking about foreign currency loans and everyday stress, and felt his arms and legs and mind working together, driving him onwards in the spring rain, and he'd felt part of burgeoning nature, part of life's force.

Maybe a memory that is good, a feeling that is tender.

Kata Choir cycles past the barn door, not stopping, clearly in a hurry. Later, he will sing for her and the whole of Valeyri. He will step forward, out of the choir, who will be humming as quietly as Kata can get them to; he will spread out his arms, embrace the hall, wrinkle his forehead, open his mouth to let his soul flow out, and he will sing: *Now all is still within the dale...*

All is still. There's silence and the memory of a feeling, and his mind is clean and clear. His eyes follow a wagtail, its tail pert in the sunshine in the doorway, and it jerks about with confidence, as if this is the perfect place to be. He, certainly, is in the perfect place. He is sitting in his barn, which he has filled over the years not with corn, but with what other people call junk, objects separated from their original purpose and waiting for a new one in what people call the real world. It's his life's mission to take things apart and reassemble them with other things. Every object here is waiting for its moment. An old door from a '66 Dodge could come in handy when you least expect it and then it would be a shame if he'd thrown it out. Stacks of old copies of *Familie* are waiting for someone to bind them into a volume, which Andrés from the museum might keep for people to leaf through. Loose sheets of poems by his uncle Guðmundur, poet of poets. A blue Volkswagen Beetle in the corner will be restored one day; maybe then he'll drive over to Jósa's, pull up outside and toot its horn – currently silent, but waiting for its moment. Just to see the look on her face, as she comes out and relives that summer evening a hundred years ago when he'd come to pick her up and they went for a drive and stopped at the head of the valley, got out and made love on a mossy spot, on a woollen rug in the colours of the Icelandic flag. And then a week later they went and made love in that old church, of all places, in front of the Saviour with his fish and loaves of bread. Made love. Now there's a memory of a feeling.

All these bits of string, rake tines, planks, electric kettles, wax, chicken wire, chairs, multi-socket extensions, curtain fabric, zips, bolts, oil, metal – all are waiting for their moment. Cables, fuses, a back scratcher, wall fixings, glue, keys, a candlestick, a bowl, an eagle feather, pencils. A phone Sidda once gave him, which he idly took apart in order to see how it worked but couldn't be arsed to put back together. Framed photographs of Gummi and his children. All have their moment, some more than once a day. A crumpled, obsolete banknote lies next to some first day covers in an old chocolate box – it too will have its moment; as will the old curtain rings from Lalli Lár's daughter, Lára; a bicycle whose chain he'd oiled for some kid or other; a wreck of a guitar that he'd mended at some point and was thinking of giving to Kata Choir; horseshoe nails and saddles that need to be taken to the stables.

Everything has its moment. A slice of marble cake waits to be eaten. A fridge in the corner hums and reminds him that it's time for his afternoon beer. Anganóra the mouse, almost as old as Kalli, waits for the slice of bread with peanut butter he usually feeds her around this time. But there's no rush; she's fine, like everything else here.

This is where people come when they can't find the right washer or screw, because they know Kalli has all the right screws and all the washers that have ever been invented, along with nails of all sizes, timber, screw-drivers, hammers, pliers, tyres, spanners. You can always go to Kalli with any problem, and if people don't return his tools he just pops round later to their garages to fetch them himself, no fuss.

This was once Kalli and Gúndi's Body Shop. People brought their cars here for every problem. He was a sort of motorcar family doctor, even making home visits when people couldn't get them to start. Gúndi looked after the books and administration, but disappeared off to South Africa one day with all the money, leaving Kalli with the debts. But they'd been good times, always new challenges, and his barn had gradually become like a surgery for objects; people brought anything that needed mending and he fixed it, and sometimes it stayed here, forgotten.

And then he'd suddenly found himself knee-deep in employment issues, and became chairman of the local trade union because it needed somebody with a bit of guts to stand up to the Lárus mob. He was out at all hours, and when he did get home Jósa was always a bit grumpy about how little he did around the house and with their little boy, Gummi – which was hardly surprising – and it had all ended on a rather sour note.

But at least they had the boy, they had that in common. All day, he's thought so much about Jósa and the times they had together, and experienced this remembered feeling as a dull pain in his loins and chest.

But he's actually stopped doing any of it really. He doesn't deal with union matters now and no longer fixes cars except for fun. But he does collect broken washing machines and mend them, which means that anyone can turn up here and get one for free. They're lined up behind him like a happy, hopeful choir of all ages robed in various shades of white, waiting for him to step forward and spread his arms to embrace the village, like he's done all these years.

He is alone. He's sitting in the sun, the generous afternoon sun that warms and shines for ever. All is still, the evening can come. And now there are two wagtails in the middle of the doorway, fussing over something. He slumps back in his chair, his gaze resting on the busy wagtails, his eyes soft, at peace – departed.

Tales Never Told

Some tales are never told, but lie buried deep down, imperceptibly affecting the village and lending colour to its appearance – unheard whispers in the wind.

They're sitting outside in the sunshine with Fríða's dandelion wine in their glasses, the afternoon breeze on their cheeks and delight in the corners of their eyes. Fríða has brought out the CD player and Baggalútur's gentle song about the sunshine in Dakota murmurs in the background. Everything's lovely, and tonight the Valeyri Choir is giving a concert in the village hall, and they'll stand on stage and sing, softly or loudly, following Kata Choir's directions. Andrés is telling that story about when Lárentíus the local sheriff and Halvorsen the chemist argued in bad Icelandic. It was hilarious, the way those two spoke. They all listen eagerly – apart from Ásta, Fríða's taciturn friend from Reykjavík; she finds it hard to keep her mind on the story and instead contemplates the splash of the surf, the shape of the mountain, the clattering of a motorboat, a fly that hovers over the dandelions and then suddenly changes its mind and buzzes straight through an open window into the house next door. She feels alone.

A village is not just the movement of the surf and a life of work, the clattering of a motorboat, or dogs that lie in the sunshine with their heads on their paws. It's not only the smell of the sea, oil, guano, life and death, the fish and the funny house names. It's also a chronicle that moves softly through the streets, preserving an elemental image of the village created piece by piece over the course of centuries. This is us, what we are like, the people of Valeyri, we here, we. Everybody knows certain chapters of this chronicle: the tale of Dr Jónas and his depression; the love story of Guðmundur, the poets' poet, and Katrín, and how she married Lalli Lár, his childhood friend, while Guðmundur, the poets' poet, lay dying of TB – abandoned her poet for the village king; tales of wily ghosts and capricious witches; a ship's crew miraculously saved at the eleventh hour, another who perished even though there was a dead calm out at sea; tales of missing persons and getting lost in perilous weather; stories of headstrong horses wandering off into the highlands and sightless dogs rescuing children; of the elves in the harbour-mouth cliffs, blown up as part of the harbour expansion in the herring years, and the curse that followed and made the herring disappear completely. Such tales: of women, seasonal workers, who took off their wedding rings on the way here to process the herring; of lovers' trysts in the Láfalaut hollow; of lecherous accordionists, of canny milk-truck drivers, of drunken priests and hapless herring speculators; of nicknames, place names, insults, curses and blessings... Some storytellers can go on well into the night when there's someone to listen to them. Some tales have been written down, some are only whispered after opening a bottle.

And some tales are never told.

Andrés from the museum is the one who tells these stories. Valeyri's great chronicle flows through his mind, and he knows every house and its name and every soul who ever lived here. He knows every car, every horse, every boat, nearly every visitor who's left behind a tale to tell.

He was brought up in a little house by the harbour. His father worked on old Lalli Lár's trawlers until he went into the nursing home to die, and his mother worked at the bakery. They had a small vegetable plot and a few sheep that Andrés was supposed to look after. They bought all the books they could lay their hands on. They lived to see their son go south to Reykjavík to study history at the university, but both died before he came home with his degree and Fríða – a Reykjavík girl raised in Karfavogur among poets and artists – and a baby girl, and moved into the old house, which he has restored beautifully with the help of good people. Not least among them Kalli, who looks in unasked every day to fix something or other, and then maybe tells Andrés a story he hasn't heard yet, or a new version of an old story, or yet another nickname that he's come up with (Kalli being the inventor of most of the Valeyri nicknames). They have replaced almost everything in the house – apart from the old grandfather clock, which they've kept because Andrés said that they had to listen to the remorseless ticking of time.

Fríða cooks supper for them, when she gets home having waited on tables and dealt with everything else at the Puffin apart from the cooking. She pays the bills and works out what they can afford; she chooses everything they buy, from crockery to the car, which she repairs: at one point Kalli said that she seemed determined to turn her husband into a child, but Sidda replied that Andrés was an intellectual and needed space to think.

They are different. He is short and a little chubby, and seems pleased with himself and perhaps a bit dim, like short and chubby men sometimes are, though he is neither. He's cheerful and sincere – Kalli says he's the personification of a smiley face. Sidda tells him not to say things like that. Fríða, on the other hand, has thick, curly hennaed hair; she wears tight clothes, high heels and make-up, and takes care of her appearance. Kalli says she's a babe with jowls. Sidda tells him to shut up.

Because he has an energetic and hard-working wife, Andrés can concentrate on the history of the village and the house. It's a house with a rich past, in which he and Fríða have brought up three children who have all moved south. The vegetable plot remains in its place, full of interesting herbs cultivated by Fríða. Andrés feels like a well-established tree in the right place – in his soil. Fríða makes her dandelion wine, famous all over the area, and in the evening they often have a drink out in the garden, and share it with friends and acquaintances who happen to pass by, making it a happy hour. As more people turn up, they merely fetch more tables and chairs. And now it's Midsummer Night, when all life turns into a golden moment. Having found a girl to fill in for her, Fríða has persuaded Lalli Lár to give her the day off from the restaurant, and now they are sitting in the sunshine with a glass of dandelion wine, and neighbours and passers-by and friends have joined them and Baggalútur are singing tenderly about the sunshine in Dakota. Everybody's going to the concert in the village hall later, but that's happening in a completely different dimension; now, at this moment, time is transformed and Andrés is in the middle of a tale about relations between Danish big shots in another century, Lárentíus the sheriff and Halvorsen the chemist. It's a tale of cursing and swearing and wrong declensions, and everybody is very amused.

The house attracts stories. The name, *Brimnes 1913*, is written on the wall, and it remembers everything, stores everything: love, arguments, tears, joy, loneliness – all the emotions that have raged here still live in its structure, all the words, all that has happened here – and tales never told.

He was born in this house. He has read about its previous occupants, and he occasionally wonders whether he can sense some of them, a subject he often discusses with Fríða in the mornings, while she's cooking the porridge. He hears a noise, and imagines the old woman who lived here for ages at the beginning of the last century, visualizes her in Icelandic national costume, her back ramrod-straight, her hair in thick plaits; or Thorkell the harbourmaster with a speech impediment, whom they called Skrolli; or Hafsteinn the headmaster, who lived here with another man, and nobody found fault with that arrangement whatsoever. He knows he isn't 'sensitive', but sometimes on long autumn nights he can hear creaking, knots snapping, curtains swishing. He sometimes thinks that he can sense something the house knows.

The little group sits sipping Fríða's dandelion wine, and everyone's very amused by the bad Icelandic the Danes spoke and how bad-tempered and silly they were. Apart from Ásta, Fríða's taciturn friend from Reykjavík. A minute ago she was watching a fly buzzing around the dandelions and had stopped listening to Andrés's prattling, and now she's watching the grass moving in the breeze. She stares in front of her. She's uncomfortable. She didn't sleep well last night and she isn't quite sure what to say to her friends.

Ásta! She'd been woken up by someone whispering her name, ever so quietly. She opened her eyes wide and heard her name whispered again. She couldn't see anyone. She couldn't hear any sounds of sleep coming from her friends' bedroom, couldn't hear the humming of the fridge, or any of the sounds that had sent her to sleep, apart from the ticking of the grandfather clock. She looked around and the room felt odd. Was she still asleep?

She closed her eyes and dozed for a while, till a gust of cold wind on her face startled her out of her slumber.

She looked around the room. The wood panelling on the walls had been replaced by threadbare, rose-patterned wallpaper. The blue chest of drawers in the corner was gone and in its place stood a chair with shabby red upholstery. Sitting in it, cross-legged, was a young woman, slim, with long, tangled hair. She was staring straight through Ásta. She wore a tight-fitting dark-blue dress and gave off a strong whiff of the sea. Ásta could neither go back to sleep nor get up. She couldn't utter a sound. Eventually, she managed to tear her eyes away from the young woman and looked towards the door: it stood open, admitting a faint light. She was sure that she'd shut the door before going to bed. The clock struck three. The floor was covered with what seemed to be drab, worn lino. She glanced at the chair again. The young woman had disappeared, but the smell was just as strong as before. She could hear the cries of Arctic terns.

Without thinking, she climbed out of bed and walked across the room. It took an age. On the floor lay a mat with a faded pattern. Outside she saw a cloudy sky. She was awake, she knew that; and she was here, she knew that. But did she really know? And where was 'here'? Tomorrow was Midsummer Day, she knew that too – so she had to be awake, here and now. But she still wasn't sure. She walked slowly down the hallway with the worn lino, in time with the ticking of the clock; barefoot, she felt the chill of the stone underneath the lino. She shivered, she was freezing. An ice-cold breeze was blowing through the open front door. In the living room a small, green lamp cast its light on the young woman, now sitting on the sofa with a small child on her lap, holding it tight and silently rocking it. Ásta could see that it was dead – or, she thought, maybe she just knew it instinctively. The young woman looked up suddenly and her eyes met Ásta's, sparkling ice-blue eyes.

It seemed to Ásta that the woman was pleading with her. Perplexed, she looked behind her, into the green-and-white-tiled kitchen. A man was sitting at the table, head buried in his hands. She cried out but didn't wake herself up – she clearly wasn't asleep. They didn't hear her. She was alone, trapped between dimensions. Something dreadful had happened here. She had to tell Andrés and Fríða about it, but she didn't know how to, because the only way to do that was to wake herself up – but if she wasn't asleep she couldn't wake up. She looked again into the living room. The young woman with the ice-blue eyes and the dead child had disappeared, along with the green lamp, and everything was dark. The house had returned to normal: the parquet floor, the pictures on the walls, the light hanging from the ceiling, Fríða's needlework on the chair, waiting for a new day. Only the ticking of the clock remained the same. She looked down – she was standing on the parquet. Underneath it the earth. The kitchen was dark and she heard the fridge's soothing hum. The front door was closed. She went to the window and looked out into the bright, living night. Up on the breakwater stood an old man, staring out to sea.

This morning when she woke up, she thought that the smell of the sea from last night was still in her room. But perhaps it had been there all along – it wasn't far to the ocean, after all. She went into the kitchen, where her friends wished her good morning. When they asked how she'd slept, she said without thinking, 'Well, thank you.' She drank the morning coffee, and helped herself to Fríða's delicious bread rolls and jam, all home-made. As they ate breakfast, she asked Andrés about people who'd lived in the house before them.

'There were many others,' he said, pleased that she'd asked. 'There was Skrolli, for instance – I haven't told you about him. He had this speech defect, and once…'

'Did a couple ever live here? With a small child?'

'Well, yes, of course. Mum and Dad, for instance, when I was little. Then, later, me and Fríða with our kids.'

'Did a child ever die here?'

He stared at her, taken aback.

'No, not that I know of,' he said. 'I don't think so. And I've probably heard everything there is to hear and read all that's been written about this place. If something like that had happened, I'd know about it.'

'Could a couple have lived here whom you don't know much about?'

'Well, um, let me think… of course, yes… there was that couple who rented the house for a short while during the herring years. They emigrated to Australia. Sigurður, he was called. And Emilía. I know very little about them, though. Truth be told, the only thing I managed to dig up was that he'd gone to Australia, and I assume she went with him.'

Now she's listening to Andrés talk about Halvorsen the chemist and Lárentíus the sheriff – a pair of utterly insignificant Danes, long since dead – impersonating them as if they were contemporaries. A seagull soars above the shore, the one from last night. The sea ripples bright blue in the sunshine. A boat glides steadily through the waves, heading for harbour, its engine clattering. Sunshine speckles the mountain. Stacked neatly against the house next door are several rolls of roofing felt, along with some timbers painstakingly arranged and covered with a tarpaulin. Stockfish are drying on wooden racks down by the sea. A woman pushing a pram appears on the path; she smiles at them and they cheerfully wave back. She's probably one of the Poles from the block of flats on the outskirts of the village. The garden is full of dandelion clocks and their seeds fill the air. The lawn needs mowing; maybe she should offer to do it – Fríða can't manage everything and Andrés clearly doesn't lift a finger. The friends are all laughing heartily as he finishes the story, and he sips his wine, contented.

In the brief silence that follows she hazards a question: 'Do any of you know anything about a child who died here, some time ago?'

There's a silence.

'Why do you ask?' says Kalli's wife, Sidda, putting her glass down.

'I don't... I dreamed...'

She doesn't know how to continue the sentence. She can't quite bring herself to tell them what happened last night.

'As I said this morning, Sigurður and Emilía are the only previous occupants I don't know much about,' Andrés replies, 'and there's definitely no record of their having had a child.'

Everyone is silent, and he adds, 'All I know is they went to Australia.'

'No, listen, this is what it is,' says Fríða finally, slapping her thighs as if to indicate the end of the discussion. 'If you dreamed that some people here had a child who died, then the child represents our republic, Iceland – in other words, the couple's dream of a life here in Iceland. That dream died when they decided to go to Australia.'

She looks around triumphantly and everybody nods.

'You should never take dreams literally,' she adds. 'You have to interpret them.'

'I suppose you could say that goes for many of us too,' ventures a quiet man with a wrinkled brow. 'I mean, that the Icelandic republic is for us a child who died.'

They all look thoughtful, nod gravely and quickly have another drink in case they should think of something that might deepen this discussion even further.

Sidda gives Ásta a curious look. 'Is that what you dreamed? That there were people here with a dead child?'

'Yes, something like that. Just nonsense, probably.'

Sidda smiles. 'Yes, one dreams so many things.' Then suddenly she lifts her arm and waves to a young woman cycling past; her smile widens and she shouts, 'Hey, Kata! See you later!'

Baggalútur are singing about the sunshine in Dakota: *After I am dead and done / and earth decays my bones / a lovely sight will be the sun / shining on my headstone.* Andrés stretches and says, 'Hey, Sidda, what about Kalli? Wasn't he going to join us?'

'Yes, he should be here by now. He's probably got his head inside one of his washing machines and has forgotten all about us.'

'Well, I'll wander over to the barn and see what he's up to. But help yourselves to more drink.'

Fríða reaches for the nearest bottle, uncorks it with a flourish and briskly tops up their glasses. They sip at the wine and smack their lips, sighing with pleasure. Ásta smiles. This conversation's not going anywhere. She feels Fríða's gentle touch on her arm. A duck waddles past with her trail of ducklings and she realizes that the dream was really about her own intense longing for a baby, and how it's too late now, and how she no longer has life under control. She looks across at the slope to the east of the house, watching the grass rippling in the breeze, the same gentle breeze that plays on her cheeks and neck. She sees the dandelions – some young and bold, others already fluffy dandelion clocks – and next to them carpets of four-leaf clover.

Búft

A fly buzzed across Reverend Sæmundur's face, disturbing his sleep. It landed on his duvet, where it briefly darted about, got bored and took to the air again, zipped past his forehead, then around his nose and finally onto his ear. He mumbled and swatted at it, and it did a little circuit round the bed before landing and starting to crawl up his arm. The fly seemed determined to rouse him, almost as if it had turned into the golden plover from that poem, telling him to 'wake up and work'. But it was only a little fly. Sæmundur could hear a real plover out on the moors, happily calling *tyu-wee* as if it wasn't thinking about him at all. It had its own life to bother about.

He felt the sun hot on his temples, intrusive as an overfriendly relation. It drilled into his head, into his consciousness. He had a headache. Saliva was smeared on his sweaty pillow. He remembered where he was and where he had been. In the same place, and yet not. He was here now, though. Friday. Midsummer Day.

He'd slept through the whole day. He hadn't gone to bed till the early hours, that much he remembered. He'd slept through midday, although he'd planned to look in on that old widow, and the afternoon, when he'd meant to put together a few words for tonight's concert. What did he have to say about choral singing? *O God, my heart is fixed; I will sing and give praise*, it says in the Psalms. He opened his mouth and *tra-la-la*ed quietly to himself for a moment. He sounded like the buzzing fly, which took his singing as a signal for another attempt to get him out of bed.

He lay for a while watching the creature circling above his head. From outside came the distant sound of a song about sunshine in Dakota. He thought about the sunshine. He thought about all this sleeping in the baking-hot sun, this summer light on duties, his ministry, his life. He took a look at himself.

The mingled stench of tobacco and beer pervaded the atmosphere like a curse. Last night he'd drunk the best part of two six-packs – the entirety of his strict, self-imposed weekly ration – and smoked a whole packet of cigarettes. He licked his lips, swallowed, and reflected on his smoking and drinking. Then the night's online activities came into his head and he felt himself grow pale inside.

He was here – here and now. Friday, Midsummer Day, and there were things to do. He was lying in his bedroom, so had evidently managed to take off his clothes and get into bed. He hadn't phoned Kata Choir last night and had not gone round to her house and tried to get her to let him in. Not this time. He remembered that, and was immediately seized by an odd feeling of pride, that he had done so well; he deserved a medal. Earlier in the summer, he'd howled outside her window until Kalli came and shooed him back home. But now was here and now. The window was open and the curtains drawn. The faraway sounds of summer wafted in and a gentle, carefree breeze brought him the scent of sea and flowers, despite all the depravity in here: the ash, the grey odour of smoking and beer-drinking.

Why wasn't he wandering among flowers? Or at sea, sailing in the wind bestowed unto us by God Almighty, Creator of Heaven and Earth? Or among birds, celebrating creation? Why was he addicted to sin? *For that which I do I allow not*, he muttered to himself. *For what I would, that I do not; but what I hate, that do I...* He reached for his well-thumbed Bible and leafed through the Psalms as if to gain strength, or to get an idea for his speech later: *Hear my cry, O God; attend unto my prayer. From the end of the earth will I cry unto thee, when my heart is overwhelmed...* He closed the book. He had been called to this place. Or had he? And by whom? Did God think about him at all – wasn't He just busy with His own stuff?

Many came *from* Valeyri. For instance, that rock star who stayed in his parents' old house for a week every summer, and always alerted the press to it; the celebrity dentist from Hafnarfjörður; Jói and Anna's daughter, famous for her business sense; the fish factory elite. But very few came *to* Valeyri. Apart from him, there were only Dr Jónas, who shut himself away in his surgery and never spoke to anybody, and of course Kata Choir. Maybe he should marry Kata Choir. Maybe Kata Choir would move in here and deliver him from evil.

When he goes shopping, he doesn't know anybody – but everyone knows him. The locals gave him a warm enough welcome at the time, and yet they always treat him like a guest, rather than a vicar. They're always talking about Kjartan, his predecessor, and his wife, Árný, who had been the local nurse since time immemorial. Dr Jónas always let her talk to the patients and preferably treat them too. While old Reverend Kjartan had been the sun that shone on everyone here, Árný was the rays of that sun, which still warmed people now. She knew everyone's ailments and alleviated all suffering; she sat with the grieving, visited the elderly, and turned up at all family celebrations, where she would sit in the middle of the parlour with a glass of sherry and tell everybody, 'I feel as if I own a little bit of you, my dear' – because she had indeed delivered everybody. They thought Reverend Kjartan's sermons monumentally dull, even incoherent, and his interpretation of scripture fanciful – despite the fact that his sermons usually concerned whatever was currently the talk of the village. Such as the time Lalli Puffin broke his leg while on the booze and Kjartan shamelessly exploited the occasion by saying that Lalli had been trying to clamber onto the camel's back in order to get through the eye of the needle – and Lalli had joined in the laughter.

The fly was on Reverend Sæmundur's face again. It had buzzed busily around his forehead before landing on his nose as if wanting to tickle it. Irritated, he jumped out from under his duvet and sat for a while on the edge of the bed, naked. He hung his head. *The good that I would...* he thought. *The good that I would...*

For a moment, the fly seemed to have disappeared, but then he spotted it crawling up the window as if wanting to escape and brag to the plover about having thrown the priest out of bed. He reflected on his life and his sins. Finally, he heaved himself to his feet and moved slowly and purposefully towards the kitchen, as if in control of himself and his situation. He opened the fridge, fished out a litre-bottle of Diet Coke and greedily drank. He went to the bathroom, peed for a long time, flushed the loo and, standing in front of the mirror, extended his hand and shook it, saying solemnly, *Yes, Ólafur, this is indeed a very happy day.* He turned on the shower and stood under its spray for a good while, intoning *The Lord be with you...* He felt the living water on his head and brow, and thought about the well of water springing into everlasting life, and told himself that he'd been permitted to drink from that spring and would never thirst hereafter.

He turned off the shower. He shaved, applied after-shave lotion and deodorant, brushed his teeth, gelled his thick, fair hair and combed it back, inspected himself in the mirror – he looked pious but good-natured, friendly yet responsible – and then opened the bathroom window. Outside, the afternoon was filled with the sound of lawn-mowers, the clattering of a motorboat, giggling children on trampolines – the sounds of summer. He went back into the bedroom and put on his trousers and a shirt, which he buttoned carefully and tucked in neatly. He took his mobile out of his jacket pocket and dialled Sigga the mayor's number; her husband, Ólafur, was chairman of both the parish council and the choir. He didn't want to ring Kata Choir herself; she wouldn't answer, not after the other day. For the briefest of moments he stood, phone in hand, and reflected on sin and the commandments, water, death and the life he lived, but then said, loudly and decisively, 'Yes, good morning!… Ha ha ha, tell me about it!' and abruptly ended the call. He strode purposefully into the kitchen and took a can of beer out of the fridge. He fetched cigarettes from the cupboard, and put them and the beer on his desk in the living room. He paused to caress the cold, damp can before returning to the kitchen to get a wet cloth and a clean glass. He wiped the desk and emptied the overflowing ashtray into the bin, rinsed it and dried it with kitchen paper. He fetched a bottle of Gammel Dansk and a shot glass and placed them next to the beer. At the window he caught sight of Kata Choir going past on her bicycle, wearing a white dress with blue polka dots, as beautiful as the life force itself. He watched her until she disappeared from view like a light going out and then drew the curtains.

He thought that it would be a shame to miss the concert tonight. And then it occurred to him that this very thought showed that he wasn't, after all, indifferent to *every*thing. He sat down at the desk with the clean ashtray, the fresh packet of cigarettes and a lighter, the beer and the Gammel Dansk. He switched on the computer and slowly poured beer into the glass and spirit into the shot glass; took the first sip of beer before the froth had subsided, but to show self-control held off the Gammel Dansk for now; lit a cigarette, inhaled and slowly exhaled; took another sip, emptied the glass and refilled it. He opened his iTunes library, selected the Stones' *Let It Bleed* and opened the internet browser. Strains of 'Midnight Rambler' filled the room and he felt a tingling in his loins.

He has arrived at the other side. In a parallel reality, a second life. At the table sits a blonde in a low-cut dress, whom he instantly nicknames Golden Miss although she's given herself the pseudonym Iofel, and he sings to himself: *The Golden Miss wants a big French kiss...* There's a bald, dark-skinned bloke with rings on every finger who calls himself Leonard and an older woman in a flowery dress; she played here all last night under the name Abba. Finally there's a slimy character who reminds him a bit of his friend Dalmann from the Theology faculty, but this one calls himself Old Nick. He was here all last night too. They seem to come in a pair, Old Nick and Abba, and he imagines them as a long-married couple, rather respectable despite having come here to the online casino. He knows that they don't like him staring at Golden Miss. 'Ah, good afternoon! And how do you do, dear madam?' he says loudly, in a deep, solemn voice, and immediately begins to jig in his seat in time with the Stones' dirty blues. The Reverend Rock.

His pseudonym is Búft, after what his medieval name-sake Sæmundur the Learned had called himself when, as the legend goes, he'd forgotten his name after three years of studying under the Devil in the Black School. Still, he'd managed to outwit Satan in the end and escape. Sæmundur thinks that adopting this name is scholarly and clever, and suggests that he's perfectly capable of dealing with the dark forces, over there on the internet.

They don't bet large sums. He imagines Iofel coming on to him. *Golden Miss no coaxing needs, to share a smoke with Sæmi...* His loins tingle. He feels the gambler in himself, the sinner. With each sip, with each drag, he feels his inner bastard spreading out like pins and needles, gradually taking over his whole being. He takes a swig, belches and grunts in time to the music. The dark bloke, Leonard, bluffs wildly and soon loses all credibility. Abba, the old woman, is keeping her powder dry, but Old Nick is unpredictable, despite looking like Dalmann, who was the very image of piety.

Reverend Búft empties his shot glass in one and pours himself another; he gets a fresh can of beer, lights another cigarette and gradually gets more and more engrossed in the game. Sometimes nothing happens for hours on end and then suddenly something does and you have to seize the moment. That's the art of it. He recalls last night's game. There were more people playing then and some had lost heavily. Not him, he knows what he's doing. He's no Reverend Daredevil, he's Reverend Careful. A solid, respectable, reliable gambler.

Boring. Like Reverend Dalmann. Dullman. Should one be reverenddullmanly? Shouldn't one bluff? Old Nick and Abba – they're the key players – they were both with him last night and what did they see? Reverend Careful. And if he were unexpectedly to make a big bet, they would think that he really had something. He has two eights.

Reverend Bluff bets more than half of everything he owns.

Golden Miss folds, and he thinks he can feel her nylon-clad foot sliding gently up his calf and see her lips part for his benefit. The dark-skinned bloke folds. Old Nick folds. There's a pause while he waits for the old woman to make up her mind. Then he gets a sign: she'll see his hand.

She has two tens. He senses her invisible smirk and a belly laugh from Old Nick. The stockinged foot abandons his calf. The game continues and he manages to scrape together small amounts by becoming boring and earth-bound. All of a sudden he remembers his life on this side and decides to ring Sigga and Óli and call in sick – a virulent flu bug; he tries out his husky flu-voice: *Na na na… Hello, how are you, Reverend Búft here… uh yes, had to take to my bed… tell me about it…* He picks up the phone, presses the redial button and listens as it rings at the other end. The music throbs, but he doesn't hear it. As he waits, he discards his hand and gets a new one. He tries to remember what he plans to say about the flu and the concert later and the mercy of Our Lord Jesus Christ. And then, suddenly, he realizes that he's holding four aces. A bright light flashes on inside him.

He's holding four aces. Stunned, he slowly puts the phone down. Four aces. That means he can win the pot. He can win fantastic sums. He's bound to. He's holding four aces. You can play poker every day for twenty years and never get four aces. It's like seeing the Beatles in concert, the Fab Four, he thinks. This is the only chance he'll get on this earth. He downs his beer, pours a Gammel Dansk, downs that and lights another cigarette, humming along to the chorus of 'You Can't Always Get What You Want'. He tried to bluff only a short time ago, so if he bets large again they'll definitely think he's gone off his head, is drunk or stuck in bluff mode, and they'll all see him. He double-bluffs. He risks everything. He doesn't hear the phone ringing, he doesn't hear Jagger and the chorus... but Golden Miss's gaze is almost tangible, and again the nylon-clad foot has begun to stroke his leg, this time travelling all the way up to his crotch. He's on fire.

He risks everything. His month's wages, the overdraft, the mortgage, the car, the Visa account, electricity, central heating, his life, health and happiness. If he wins now he may be saved. Then he can turn over a new leaf and become a new man. Though he knows deep inside that he'll always come back here to look down from his life's precipice into the abyss, because here on the cliff's edge he feels like a man. Here, he feels as if he's living. Soaring.

Old Nick sees him. Abba too. He shows his cards and the pictures of Iofel and Leonard immediately disappear from the screen. The chorus drones on incessantly about getting what you want in this life. Búft gazes into the abyss. He's on the edge of his life's precipice.

He downs a beer and opens another can. The phone's still ringing. The music pounds on.

Only three of them are left in the game. He examines their avatars while he waits. He blinks and they've changed. Before, Abba's mouth had been puckered in disapproval, but not now. She's no longer judging him. She's wearing a white dress, and her hair is white and curves charmingly around her soft cheeks, not up in a tight bun as before – it looks a bit like a dove – and her smile is unbelievably peaceful, omniscient, as if she knows all his sins and peccadilloes, his innermost thoughts, delusions and dreams, knows him beyond word and deed, and can make him stir like grass in the breeze or send him off out into the world like seeds from a dandelion clock. Old Nick's mouth is stuck in a rictus grin that grows ever more manic. Strands of grey hair are combed over his bald patch. He has a fat face with a double chin and a cold sore on his bottom lip; his skin looks as if he eats too many rubbishy sweets, drinks too much cheap wine from a box, smokes too much pot. He has a ring on the fourth finger of his right hand with a scrawl on it, some indecipherable squiggle. No, it's a picture, a picture of a fly with wriggling feet. Rings with flies on them, black, green, red, on every finger. Reverend Sæmundur, his face distorted, raises his arms in a gesture of prayer as the music booms and his phone rings. His life is in their hands, everything depends on which way the game ends, here on his life's precipice – this he realizes as the alcoholic haze briefly clears. Everything is at stake: he's either lost or saved for ever.

He's holding four aces, but this doesn't matter. He knows that people don't always get what they want, but, on the other hand, they do sometimes get what they need. He realizes that, whatever happens, untold challenges await him: a long journey down a stony road, across scree and gravel, through fire and burnt-out cities, shadowed days, disgrace, and a deep valley, until he reaches the gates of darkness.

Aroma of Ashes

Sunlight pours in through the west-facing door. Ólafur watches the rays dancing in his wine as he recalls a great Dixieland band he saw on YouTube yesterday. He takes another sip, the memory of it makes him smile, and he begins to tell the others about it in a soft, almost matter-of-fact voice, and the three of them watch him, smiling. But there's unrest in the air.

He says he can't remember what it was called – but it was on YouTube, he repeats somewhat solemnly, as if that was an important fact, in itself a little funny, as he realizes with a new-found sensitivity brought on by the wine. He repeats, almost sternly, 'YouTube, you know.' He pauses very briefly, to admire the sun's rays dancing playfully around his glass and reflecting from the walls of their bright and beautiful living room, but then describes in remarkable detail how the clarinettist, a pretty girl, had raised one foot as she played, how the trombonist rolled his eyes, how the scrawny trumpeter held his instrument as if he could scarcely lift it, and how the drummer grinned and twirled his drumsticks as the stocky double bass player spun his instrument around like a dance partner in a polka. He was so amusing, that double bass player. On YouTube.

Ólafur is overbearingly tall, slim and fair-haired, boyish despite being nearly sixty, but without grace. He stoops and always moves a bit like a puppet; now that he's had a few glasses of white wine he seems to be lifting his arm not of his own accord, but as if someone's pulling a string as he takes a sip – which he does quite frequently, though he's singing with the choir later, down at the village hall. He's thoughtful and cautious, and nobody blames him for the fact that the bank collapsed, or was rescued at the last minute, or was transformed into a new bank, or whatever it was that happened, nobody really knows. The general view is that it was the fault of the global financial crisis, because Ólafur has been a rock to the entire community, even though some people, mainly journalists, actually, and bloggers from down south, asked questions about the huge loans the bank had made to the Valeyri Fish Factory, and to what extent those had been to blame for the bank's collapse, and exactly what the relationship was between the branch manager and the factory board.

All this, of course, is easily answered. They are a unit. The people sitting here are a molecule; Óli and Sigga, Jói and Anna. They would always be as one.

Perhaps one day Óli will have to answer for what happened, but Sigga thinks that in that case he should also be allowed to talk about the role he has played here in the community, as confessor and saviour. How he's sat in his office with countless villagers, sorting out car loans and mortgages and hire-purchase contracts and debt demands, helping them to unravel their financial entanglements. And never made a fuss. Do the scandal junkies down south ever talk about that? Do the papers down south ever mention how he has sat here and calmed people, advised them, pointed them back in the right direction, lent them money and made sure that they didn't rashly embark on careless investments that could actually wait? Sigga feels that if he were to be prosecuted for approving loans to the Valeyri Fish Factory, which certainly were instrumental in the bank's collapse – or whatever happened – it should be easy for him to explain his actions in a professional way: how he'd acted on the best available information from head office down south, provided by people he was confident he could trust, how he was misled by people who had themselves been misled by people. She knows all this because in the evenings, when it is quiet, they snuggle into bed and talk to each other, the branch manager and the mayor, and he tells her everything and she listens while she caresses the small of his back and his hair and thighs and bottom and ends up masturbating him so that all the day's frustrations spurt out of him.

But they aren't thinking about banking crises or service jobs now. Later on, they're going to enjoy a concert in which they'll all be singing. The white wine is chilled, and the breeze is warm now that the cool of the late afternoon has passed, and the sun's rays are dancing on the walls, drunk on the wine in which they've been frolicking. And there was that great Dixieland band, Ólafur said, he'd seen on YouTube yesterday when he was looking for some decent jazz in Slovakia for Einar to go and hear when he goes over to Trnava to sing in the opera.

Ólafur takes another sip of the refreshingly cool, slightly sharp wine. 'I think they were Czech or from around there or something, unless they were from YouTube?' he says thoughtfully. 'And they played, you know, Dixieland… you know, it's so cheerful, such fun. And they were so lively. Especially the double bass player, he was a hoot. I'd quite like to see them – listen, guys, shall we pop over to Trnava to see Einar in *The Gypsy Princess* and take in this band at the same time?'

The sun-drenched wine has clearly gone to his head and he's repeating himself; it's as if he's temporarily lost control, is suddenly drunk. But Sigga knows that it won't last long, because as soon as he becomes aware of it he'll have a glass of water and keep drinking water till he's regained control over himself.

He is like that.

The phone rings upstairs, but he doesn't seem to hear it. He waves his arms around and says in a strange voice, 'I think… I…?'

A gentle breeze drifts in from outside – the smell of the sea. Anna and Jói occupy the sofa. Sigga stands in the middle of the room, looking at Óli, thinking about him. She hesitates as if unsure whether to run upstairs to answer the phone, fetch the food, or stay and listen to the story. There's unrest in the air, maybe because of the phone, maybe it's drifting in from outside with the squeals of the children on the trampoline, the motorboat's clattering and the squawking of the seagulls, or maybe it's triggered by something between them, because these four go back a long way. They affect each other, and there are many things they know about each other and various things they don't know about each other – despite being a molecule. And things they don't know that they know about each other.

With gentle eyes he looks at his Sigga and then at Jói – then fixes his gaze on Anna. 'I think…' he says in a hoarse voice. 'I…?'

And the sunlight flows in from the west – there's plenty more of it, and suddenly it's as if the evening won't be coming at all, not until maybe sometime in the autumn.

Now and again the dying breeze billows a white curtain with lazy sensuality. A heavily laden honey bee buzzes on the patio. From outside come the giggles of children jumping on trampolines, mixed with the strident sounds of the redshank and the winnowing of the snipe, the ringing of the telephone, and Roy Orbison crooning about loneliness on the CD player in the background. The others smile at Óli. They know him and they know that this will pass. He's never drunk for more than three or four minutes at most. He will probably take the phone call himself. They're usually for him.

This is what their lives are like. They are a molecule. They are a unit. Anna and Sigga are the very bestest of friends in the whole world and Jói and Óli are best mates, and they were all here together playing catch and 'One, Two, Buckle My Shoe' on the streets, got confirmed together and attended Akureyri High School together, having paired themselves off almost automatically – *Thirteen, fourteen, maids a-courting* – the petite dark one with the tall fair-haired bloke and the small, dark bloke with the tall blonde – and they went to Copenhagen together for a few years at university, came back and built their houses side by side, and had their children one after the other, who were brought up together and played catch and 'One, Two, Buckle My Shoe' – and went south.

They meet at weekends and drink white wine and have something fine and exotic to eat, which they cook together, working in harmony from all kinds of recipes, and they play bridge instead of ball games outside like they used to when they were kids. Sometimes they go for a ride on the horses that Kalli looks after for them. They are life partners. Sometimes they have guests – Andrés and Fríða, Árni Going Places, who lives in the old doctor's house, and Jósa, or Kalli and Sidda, Árný the nurse, and Jói's old mother, Lára, who is Lalli Lár's daughter and the only one of their parents still alive. But then they can't invite Lára's brother, Lalli Puffin, because he and Lára aren't on speaking terms.

Sometimes they sing together in harmony to the accompaniment of Óli's maudlin (and inaccurate) accordion playing, and on Thursday evenings they gather here, at Sigga and Óli's, to listen to the symphony concert from Reykjavík on the radio; some of the villagers poke fun at them for this and call Ólafur 'Óli Smartypants'. But how else would the four of them have got to know Mahler and Rimsky-Korsakov?

They go on cultural trips, sometimes down south but more often abroad, because Reykjavík feels like an unnecessary stopover. They sometimes joke that Valeyri is more of a city than the capital; it's got a café, a choir and a harbour bustling with activity – and druggies in dark corners. They've taken weekend breaks to all the big European cities, always meticulously planned: museums and theatres and other significant buildings before lunch, after which Anna and Sigga go off to buy presents for the grandchildren in H&M and hunt for bargains and be the bestest friends in the whole world, while Óli and Jói have a beer at a pavement café or a bar and talk. Jói quickly gets tipsy and starts confessing his sins and Óli nods, interjects the odd encouraging and sympathetic word, shakes his head, laughs, sighs, massages his friend's aura. And of course they also have to keep up with Óli and Sigga's son, Einar, as he does the rounds of minor European opera houses performing roles in Italian operas, not leading roles, admittedly, but not the smallest ones either; he often gets an aria, which he always makes the most of. The men go on trips to watch Manchester United and sit, wearing their team shirts, in the supporters' stand with other Icelanders from out in the sticks, and sing along with the rest of them, sheepishly inebriated and happy. Afterwards, they go to a bar and Óli becomes a bit woozy for a minute or two and nods sympathetically, while Jói gets completely plastered and confesses all. They also keep the local football team going. It's called Svarri, after Valeyri's mountain; they've bought players from here and there, and a trainer, and as a result the team has occasionally made it into the top league, hovering there for a short while but soon dropping down again.

This is what their lives are like. They are children of the sun and they radiate prosperity, with their complexions tanned just enough without looking weathered, their clothes, their jewellery, how they carry themselves. Once dark-haired, Jói now has a ring of grey stubble surrounding his bald patch, and although it's just stubble on the head of a bald bloke there's something about it that looks intentional, as if designed by an Italian barber; his neck is thick enough to indicate limitless sexual drive and he has large, strong hands that could create countless tools to change the world, and he caresses everything within his vicinity as if to sense its structure and possibilities: cabinets, wood, stones, artefacts – and women. Every woman he meets becomes like a new mirror in which to see his own reflection, a hint of another kind of life which he must savour before carrying on with his own. He is restless, strides about, constantly tucking in his shirt, almost threateningly; he seems possessed of the entrepreneur's unwavering charm and makes people feel as if he is about to build something magnificent. Also dark-haired, Sigga is small and broad-hipped – child-bearing would have left her chubbier, if she hadn't constantly counted the calories – and, like Jói, has an efficient and successful manner, is quick-witted (which everyone likes), sensitive and kind. She and Jói are related, second cousins once removed. She knows all there is to know about her children and grandchildren, because she knows how to ask the right questions and draw the right conclusions. When she was five she decided that Anna, who lived three houses away, should be her best friend because she was so beautiful, with blonde curls, a bright smile and a gentle disposition, and since then they have met every day – the bestest friends in the whole wide world.

Three years ago, she decided to go for it when the rest of the local Independence Party committee persuaded her to lead the party in the local council elections, and she proved so popular that they achieved a clear majority and she was appointed mayor, after having worked in the school office for years.

And Anna... she sits on the sofa, so pretty, her legs crossed and her shapely fingers holding the stem of the glass in her lap, the same silky-soft sweep of blonde hair as back then, the same graceful physique, the small upturned nose and big blue eyes, the same decorous smile hiding all sorrow, repulsion, ardour – anything that might be stirring inside her. She has 365 dresses, and when she teaches the children geography and maths none of them can find it in themselves to misbehave, because it might upset her. And yet her mind is hard and her heart is cold. If her thoughts include even the slightest affection for Jói, she manages to hide it from herself.

He has stood up now, even though the story about the band on YouTube doesn't seem to have completely finished, because Óli – gazing earnestly into Anna's eyes and saying in a strange voice, 'I think... I...?' – is still waving his hands as if looking for the right words to describe exactly what tune they were playing on YouTube, that Dixieland band that was so great. Upstairs, the phone is ringing. Jói has started to tuck in his shirt, in that fierce way of his, as he paces the floor. It's a nervous habit with him, as if he thinks that his pot belly is a secret that can be hidden by a straightened-out shirt. He imagines that all his secrets are tucked in. He is restless. Returning Óli's earnest gaze, Anna notices out of the corner of her eye that Jói has lost weight and gets a strong sense that he's started smoking again, even though she hasn't smelt it on him yet. She needs to ask Sigga about this. That's how their lives interweave, that's how their mutual trust works: Jói confesses his sins to Óli, who in turn tells Sigga about them in the evenings before they go to bed, on the strict promise not to tell anybody, least of all Anna – and Sigga then tells Anna about it at the kitchen table as they hold hands, the very, very bestest friends in the whole world. This is how Anna knows about Jói's adventures on his business trips down south, about the cheating and the drinking and the gambling. And about the troubles in the Valeyri Fish Factory that he never talks about at home, unless it's to reassure her that everything's all right, just as if he were tucking in his shirt.

She knows all his secrets. She sees through him. The place he used to occupy in her heart is a cold, dead hollow where flowers once grew; an attic covered in cobwebs in a ruined palace; a freezer compartment where each new story of his adventures and follies, each new confession, is stored. In the old days, it used to be a hot place that warmed her insides wherever she went, but it all began to die twenty years ago when she was dusting his desk and came across a letter carelessly stuffed under the phone bills. From someone called Olga, it contained a drawing of him naked with his penis erect and red hearts squirting out of it; underneath, in bold, feminine handwriting, were the words *love balls* and *cutie bum* and *hot willy*. When Anna confronted him that evening as they stood side by side in the bathroom cleaning their teeth, he stopped, lowered his toothbrush and stared at himself in the mirror, aghast, and remained silent for a long time before confessing that he'd had an affair with this artist in Reykjavík who was always in the papers because of the 'happenings' she organized. Then he started pacing around the bathroom, trying to tuck in his pyjama top, howling and crying and swearing that this was nothing but a silly fling, that he was a man who needed his release but she alone was the queen of his mind, the muse at his table, the goddess, the sun, she alone owned his heart and his mind – and probably also his lungs and kidneys as well, as she sarcastically put it when reporting the conversation to Sigga, as the two of them sat in Sigga's kitchen a few evenings later. She alone mattered to him, he said – he loved her.

'So does that mean,' she asked quietly, 'that you can't treat people properly if you love them?'

He sank to his knees, crawled to her, weeping, and asked for her forgiveness, to give him another chance, he would learn his lesson, it was stupid of him to look elsewhere, a man whose wife was the most beautiful in the whole country, the goddess of light itself... She kicked him in the chest and stormed out. He fell against the bathtub and cut the back of his head, but she ignored him, put a coat on over her nightdress and went down to the shore, which was deserted apart from Smyrill the poet standing there gazing at the ocean. She raged along the water's edge and thought about what a bastard he was and whether she should start a new life down south with the children, then ten and twelve years old – she could teach just as well there as here – and find herself an eighteen-year-old lover. Then she went home to sleep. A new day dawned with a new silence.

That evening he brought her flowers, stared at her like their pet dog and enthusiastically agreed with everything she said to the children. She threw him out of the bedroom and they never again slept together. Never again did she trust him, but she knew that without her he would be lost; she continued to despise him always, but occasionally, when he looked particularly miserable, she stroked his hair or his cheek, and he would pitifully stretch his head towards her like a love-starved puppy.

And now he's back on his feet and has started tucking in his shirt, pacing the floor. This is what he does: he'll suddenly stand up, kill the conversation by completely changing the subject, start fiddling with his phone while people are talking to him. Some people think it's a sign of great energy and busyness, but Anna knows it's just lack of discipline, an inability to finish anything, whether at home or elsewhere. She'd pinned all her hopes on their daughter; she knew that Helga was different from Jói, more like her, and she'd been so happy when Jói, after discussing it with her and his mother, Lára, decided to hand over the business to Helga. In those days they sometimes talked to each other like proper people, and they agreed that Helga was the right person to take the business in a new direction, and he said as much to Óli, so Sigga had told her. Then came the collapse. It was all a misunderstanding, a bubble, a web of lies. And even though on the surface everything seemed unchanged and they had plenty of money – thanks to Sigga, she knows that he has enough cash stashed away in secret accounts – Jói doesn't do anything except sit and contemplate his navel, waiting for permission to take back control of the Valeyri Fish Factory, the place where he has known everything since he was nine years old and where he can take on any job and knows how everything should be and not be. While he waits for a decision from the resolution committee in the south, he exhausts himself pacing the floor and tucking in his shirt, committing sins and confessing them to Óli when in his cups.

There's unrest in the air. Upstairs, the phone is ringing. And yet Óli still hasn't quite finished telling his story about that band on YouTube. It seems to have ground to a halt and Sigga starts to shuffle her feet. She was about to go to the kitchen, to fetch the snack they were going to have before the concert, a salad of cold trout with dill sauce, easily digested, but now the phone has started ringing and she also thinks that maybe Óli needs to finish this YouTube story first, except maybe the story is finished, because he's stopped talking in mid-sentence and is waving his arms about as if trying to remember something, and saying so strangely, 'I think... I...?' In a week's time, it'll be forty years since he proposed to her. It was on one of those September evenings that sometimes happen in May, when greyness covers everything as if by some unknown law of nature. They'd only recently arrived from the south, after their last winter in high school. They drove into the valley, as courting couples here in Valeyri do, and he switched off the engine at the head of the valley, as you do, and sat at the wheel for a while before abruptly turning to her and saying, 'Shall we get married?'

Now and again, but only as needed, the perfectly calibrated wipers slid across the windscreen. And at that moment, popping the question, he too was perfectly calibrated and successful. She naturally didn't have to think about it and said yes straight away. She's never regretted it; their life together has been orderly and successful, with rough patches smoothed away promptly – apart from Jói's constant troubles. Then again, they'd actually created a greater empathy between them. He was not very interested in gardening or carpentry or DIY, but he was a kind soul; he went out into the street with the children when they were learning to ride a bicycle, running up and down for an hour steadying their bikes, even though they had long since got the hang of it and people were looking out of their windows, laughing at Óli Smartypants.

He was still like that, and she knew that he'd helped a lot of people at the bank, and that it wasn't his fault how it had all turned out. Actually, sometimes it was almost as if nothing had changed, even though the bank had gone bust. At least, he was still working there as he'd always done and they still had more than enough for themselves and the children. Which was just as well, because Einar's singing lessons in Vienna weren't exactly cheap and Alda had taken out a foreign currency loan (which became a nightmare when the krona devalued) to pay for that house of hers in Hafnarfjörður. She knew that Óli sometimes got upset – as she also did – about Alda and Einar having both gone away. He found it hard not to see them every day. And the grandchildren – he never talked about how rarely he got to see them, never mentioned how different things were for Jói and Anna, whose daughter, Helga, was always around and often popped in with her kids. But then she had a business here with her dad, and it wasn't surprising that she came so often – for a time, that is; the visits were, of course, not so frequent now.

The villagers still call Jói 'Jói Lára Lár', after his mother. When he took over the Valeyri Fish Factory from her, he had his own ideas about modernizing the company, which he felt had become old-fashioned and too tied to its original production values. As luck would have it, Helga had just graduated from Reykjavík University with top marks in Business Studies, and had written a dissertation on investment engineering entitled 'Optimal Utilization of Fishing Quota Rights and Blue-Ocean Opportunities for Investment in Emerging Industries'. She'd taken a job at the bank, where she set up a group that worked on restructuring company policy.

Jói felt that it was very appropriate for Helga to take over the company and to run it as her grandmother Lára had done, not least because they both had useless husbands: Jói's father had been a bedridden drunk for decades, while Helga's husband was a cute footballer who specialized in diving to win free kicks and penalties. Helga and her mates began by leveraging the quota to obtain immense loans from the bank, because they said that it would cost more not to take out loans, and by doing this they were able to maximize returns on the quota – *Get the cash off the silo and down onto the conveyor belt*, as Helga put it and Jói never tired of repeating.

Company policy was scientifically worked out, using all kinds of mathematical models, and they invested in a variety of attractive emerging ventures, besides which Jói was given the opportunity to buy into companies that particularly interested him. What did he get for his pennies? He got a car dealership in Reykjavík; a football team with a very expensive trainer from Scotland and twenty-eight players from a mix of countries; a high-tech company with grandiose plans to cultivate enzymes from thermophilic microbes which were supposed to smooth out all wrinkles. He sat in endless meetings and didn't understand a word. The money flew away and Jói kept dashing from one place to another, trying to keep up with all the goings-on in his life. Before, he had only been in charge of the fish factory, and had been faithful in a few ways: had shown up at eight o'clock every morning and kept an eye on all that happened there, from every single cod fillet to the extramarital affair between the foreman in reception and the woman in accounting. Now he was running around after his business affairs like a maniac, always in Reykjavík, unfaithful in a multitude of ways.

This was during the years in which all who wanted to believe were allowed to believe what they wanted and all who wanted to lie could lie as much as they pleased. There was only one condition: unqualified success. There was a universal public agreement that there has to be unqualified success, whatever the cost. Maybe when Jói woke up in the middle of the night with pangs of anxiety in his belly he didn't believe that he was successful, or didn't understand what success actually was, and maybe he knew deep down that he wasn't really suited to running a football team or car dealership, let alone some enzyme company, even if he did have a good degree from a Danish technical college and knew, for instance, everything about how to build a house – but he always managed to get back to sleep, because he firmly believed that nothing would happen to him. He believed that someone was watching over him. He said as much to Óli, who told Sigga, who told Anna. He believed that he would always get away with everything. That's how it had always been and he felt that it was because of his grandmother in heaven rather than his mother on earth, who always took care of paying for everything, or his wife, who put up with his excesses.

He believed that someone was watching over him. Yesterday he sat in Óli's office, and this time it was Óli who talked and Jói who listened. The bank's resolution committee in Reykjavík had informally communicated its decision to Óli. The debts were to be more or less written off – they would be absorbed by the black hole that swallowed all Icelanders' debts – and the family would regain the majority share in the Valeyri Fish Factory and would be able to go back to running the company as they'd always done.

He embraced his friend, didn't say a word, fiercely tucked his shirt in and marched out, making straight for his car. He drove, weeping, to the head of the valley. He got out and felt the breeze on his cheeks and sat down in the moss where he and Anna had made love for the first time, at the age of fifteen that summer night on a woollen rug in the colours of the Icelandic flag, after which they'd shared a Benson & Hedges he'd nicked from his mum. He thought about that moment.

He thought about himself and Anna. He thought about all the sorrow he had caused her, the silence, the coldness, the misery. He went back to the car, reached into the glove compartment and fished out the packet of cigarettes he'd kept there, untouched, for the last five years, took one out and lit it with the car's lighter. Once again he sat down in the moss. He thought that he mustn't take Anna for granted. He thanked his grandmother in heaven for her guidance and promised her that for the rest of his life he would be a worthy husband to Anna and regain her respect. The cigarette made him feel dizzy and tasted weirdly bad, and he promised himself – and his grandmother in heaven – to begin a new life with Anna by telling her that he'd started smoking again. All secrets would now be banished from their lives. Still whimpering, he solemnly rose, got into the car and drove off slowly and deliberately towards Valeyri, like a man in control of his life. On the way back he called his mother. She'd already heard the news and snorted inscrutably. When he arrived home he found that Anna had gone to bed. He stayed in the living room for a long time, clutching a glass of whisky, listening to the clinking of the ice cubes. Then he went upstairs to sleep. A new day dawned with a new silence.

His friend Óli had gone straight home after their talk, asked Sigga to come into the bedroom, told her of his conversation with Jói and, as always, asked her not to tell anybody about this – especially not Anna. She had promised not to, but as soon as he was asleep she had put on her jogging gear and gone over to Anna's, and as they walked hand in hand through the village, the very bestest friends in the whole wide world, she had told her that everything would be as it had always been.

There's unrest in the air. Upstairs, the phone is ringing. Jói has stood up. He strides across the room towards his friend, tucking his shirt into his trousers. He looks worried. Sigga is shuffling her feet as if unsure whether to go and answer the phone, fetch their pre-concert snack from the kitchen or listen to Óli's story about those Czech Dixieland players. She looks at her husband, confused. Anna sits on the sofa, her legs crossed, looking straight into Óli's eyes. She's stopped thinking about Jói, she sees only Óli, who looks straight into her eyes, with a look that tells her he has always had eyes only for her and her alone, and says in a strange voice, 'I think... I...?' and then drops his glass, which shatters into a thousand crystal fragments on the wooden floor as he grabs his chest and sinks to the floor saying hoarsely, 'I think that... that something... I'm...'

Sonata for Harmonica in C Major

Gunnar has never forgotten that morning in downtown Reykjavík, when they were teenagers. It was five or six o'clock in the morning; they had been at a party; they'd drifted around the Thingholt area as if lost – this street, that street – until they came to Amtmannsstígur, where they suddenly stopped as if they'd found the place that doesn't exist, the place where time doesn't exist. Although he doesn't talk about it, Gunnar has never forgotten that morning; the houses and gardens and cars were bathed in the morning sun, and he took his harmonica out and said, 'Wait, listen,' and began to improvise a tune. Between in-breaths, without breaking its flow, he said, 'This is for you!' Tall, slim and serious, she stood motionless and pigeon-toed, watching him. Though there wasn't a breath of wind, she pushed a lock of hair behind her ear and wrapped her parka, that green parka, around herself and crossed her arms against an imagined chill. Meanwhile the street slept: the people in the houses, the birds on the roofs, the cats under the cars. Then he saw that one of the cats had woken up and was now standing in front of him, looking at him accusingly. He brought the tune to an end with a jaunty glissando, put the harmonica back in his pocket and drew her towards him; she put her arms around his neck and they kissed in this secret place on Amtmannsstígur, the place that didn't exist. It was a morning kiss. It was a night kiss. It was their first kiss and their last kiss, their best kiss and their only kiss.

Even though they had kissed each other often.

'Remind me, how long were we together?' he says suddenly.

He's making coffee and, although his back is turned, senses how she freezes. He immediately regrets the question. He worries that it sounded too brusque, too flippant, but he doesn't know how to soften it, doesn't know how to approach her any more – doesn't know what she thinks. He concentrates on the coffee, making sure that the boiled water infuses all the grounds in the filter, he'd learned that from his dad – doing it all properly – and is aware that the tip of his tongue is sticking out of the corner of his mouth, like when he was a boy and had to make a flask of coffee for his dad and take it to him in the garage when he was ashore. Dad would glance up briefly from his work, pour himself a cup and say to him, 'Just a tick,' before taking a sip, nodding his approval and saying, 'You're getting there, son.' This morning he had looked at himself in the mirror and felt eleven years old. But he isn't eleven. He has just turned fifty. He celebrated his birthday with a few friends and colleagues, heartily and at length, and they sang, *For he's a jolly good fellow*. She hadn't been there.

Turning around, he sees that she's looking out of the window at Kata Choir cycling past, wearing a white dress with blue polka dots. She herself is in a blue jumper. After all those years abroad she probably feels the cold, despite the sun. But it's loose-fitting and he can see her collarbones. Her hair no longer falls in soft waves down to the small of her back, but is short and dyed a dark brown, making her face look harder, more tired. But she still has a big nose; still has that little wrinkle in the centre of her forehead, sitting there like a link between the halves of her brain; still has a long, soft chin that he longs to caress; still has blue eyes that can transport him anywhere on earth. She doesn't reply, doesn't say anything, just watches the woman on the bike – almost perplexed. Maybe she doesn't know the answer any more than he does and needs to think about it, or maybe she thinks that he doesn't remember that they'd been together four years, three months, five days and thirty-six minutes. Not counting the teenage years.

Maybe she feels that he shouldn't barge so clumsily into their sanctuary.

He has no idea what she thinks.

Maybe she feels that they're not the same as they used to be. They'd found each other when they were teenagers and together listened to music that her cousin in Reykjavík sent her from the record shops. It was important music,

hard music, full of screeching guitars and scraggy synthe-
sizers and agony. They sat silently and tried to understand
this desolate, metallic sound from the greyness of big
cities where everybody was unemployed. In Valeyri there
was plenty of work, as his father never tired of telling his
brother when he complained that there was *nothing* here.
These thin, nasal voices brought to Iceland on the wings
of civilization strangely suited the drizzle, the bad temper,
the isolation, the doggedness. The records spun on the
turntable in his bedroom like seductive black holes and
the two of them watched, mesmerized, until they came
to an end, the crackle stopped and the arm clicked back
automatically onto its rest, and they would sit together
for a while, silently contemplating themselves and their
life. His mother was in the kitchen, silently contemplating her dishcloths and her despair, while his brother sat
in his room banging away with a sawn-off shotgun on
his games console, although he was two years older and
should have been either on his way down south to high
school or at sea.

She only had to appear at the end of the football
pitch, motionless and pigeon-toed, for him to make an
excuse and go over to her, even if it was looking like he
was about to score a goal – he gave up everything for her.
Her parents gave her an electric guitar with a small amplifier for Christmas; his brother gave him his old guitar,
in which he'd lost interest, some kind of a child's guitar
from Korea that kept going out of tune, which meant
that he constantly had to fiddle with the pegs.

They sat in his room composing their own songs, cross-legged and facing each other. As quickly as the tunes came to them, they learned to play them on their guitars, copying each other's grips and competing to find the barre chords. Over their strumming, she sang songs and tuneless strains about the wind and about the absolutely-nothing-at-all that she experienced here, the stench, the mist and all the rubbish. He followed and embellished, and was quick to find the rhythm because it was the rhythm of her mind. They were songs of melancholy. But one was different from all the others. She improvised it on the day before one Christmas Eve, when his dad was even worse than usual, blind drunk on the living-room sofa and bellowing at the world. Because she'd just learned the C minor grip it came out gentle and wistful, and she sang it in a clear and beautiful voice.

It was called 'It'll All Be All Right'. The lyrics went like this:

It'll all be all right – it won't go wrong
It'll all be all right – just sing this song
I told you so, I told you so.

It's all all right – it's all on song
All, all, all right – just sing along.
I told you so, I told you so,
I told you so, I told you so.

She was major and he was minor. She was pigeon-toed and straight-backed, he was always going out of tune. She had brown hair, with a beautiful lustre that she achieved with daily use of the right conditioner. He had blond curls that grew in all directions, making him look ever more harmless the longer he grew his hair, even though his intention was the exact opposite. She was plucky and bold, but he felt the world was continually trying to bring them down. Nobody understood them. They drifted round the village, hand in hand, long-haired, dressed in black and, when she felt like it (which was often), wearing the same make-up. There was a rumour going round that they were smoking pot, but they didn't even know what that looked like. It was the music and the loneliness, the boredom and the longing to get away, that made them different from the others and affected how they behaved, talked, dressed. Sometimes they lay fully clothed in each other's arms with the remorseless rock music pounding over them like a sermon. Sometimes they stroked each other's hair, cheeks, necks, foreheads and backs. Sometimes they kissed, tasting and caressing each other. She said she loved him. He closed his eyes, clasped her ever more tightly to him, running his hands urgently down her spine. All around them the kids had begun sleeping with each other, they knew, but their love was different. They were different. Nobody understood them. They planned to go away as soon as they could, to where the music was, the clothes, the style, all the words and voices – south, where civilization's migratory birds spread their wings.

One morning he came out of his room and found his brother hanging from a beam in the living room. His brother was seventeen years old and had finally decided what to do with his life: end it. That evening, while his mother was on the phone to his dad out at sea, they lay arm in arm against the tall, grey acoustic panel he'd set up in his room, speaking in whispers. She told him how her stepfather constantly tried to press up against her while pretending to reach for something behind her, how he hovered around while she got undressed in the evening or had a bath; how disgusting and repulsive he was, and that she couldn't even tell her mother about it but had to get away before he got any worse. He told her about his brother, who had always been apathetic and depressed, and glued to his games console; and about his dad, how controlling and aggressive he was, his devastating boozing when ashore, drunk and ranting at the supper table; and about the relentless unhappiness in this home that had finally ended in a knot tightened around a throat. Together, they tried to find ten reasons that made life worth living. They presented their pain to each other, they took that pain and scrutinized it together and took care that it didn't burn them. They brought it into the light so that it would go away. They saw how ugly it was and small. But it didn't go away.

They were sixteen and nobody understood them. It was only a matter of time before they would leave this place to go and do something worthwhile, meet people who weren't idiots. She drifted around wearing jumpers and shirts that had belonged to her father, who had died when she was five. He wore a duffel coat and black T-shirts with Japanese cartoon figures grinding their teeth. Sometimes they wore each other's clothes, and when she felt like it (which was often) she would put black eye make-up on them both and they would go outside like that and walk hand in hand down to the harbour and back. Then they were invincible.

'Remind me, how long were we together?'

Maybe this sounds, Gunnar thinks, as if I'm just chatting about something that doesn't really matter that much.

Maybe it sounded as if everything was all right.

Maybe it sounded as if he hadn't fallen from a height of 6,000 feet without a parachute and crashed brutally onto the rocks below when she dumped him.

Maybe it sounded as if she hadn't ripped both his arms off when she left him, hadn't pulled his hair out and torn off his scalp, hadn't taken his heart and stamped on it and cast it to the bottom of the ocean and left him on the outermost promontory of Grímsey with open wounds for the ravens to feast on.

She sits opposite him, gazing out of the window. They haven't seen each other for thirty years – since she went abroad and left him here embracing her absence and all the words she'd given him. She didn't come back, for her it was enough to write him a letter, such a sweet letter. She sits here with him in the kitchen and once again it feels like the blue colour of the corner cupboard is there purely because her eyes are blue. It's as if the kitchen once again took its shape from her presence, its light from her smile. She has tucked one leg under the other, like she used to do, and she's watching Kata Choir cycle past.

'Who's that?' she finally asks, ignoring his question. 'On the bike over there?'

He's relieved that she's acting as if nothing happened and almost babbles as he starts telling her all the village gossip that they'd so heartily detested back in the day.

'Kalli Skjól – Uncle Kalli – was at a conference in Reykjavík a few years back representing the Valeyri Trade Union – that's just him and Sidda, remember – and found himself in some pole-dancing club with a bunch of union mates…'

'You know, I don't think I want to hear this.'

'No, wait. He sits down with some fat trade unionists to watch naked birds dance and stuff like that, but then one of the dancers sits down next to him and they start talking. And you know what Kalli is like, more than anything he's a decent chap and a car mechanic, he can't stand problems, and it's like when he's fixing a car, he needs to solve them. He sees she's not very happy and he gets this utterly unbelievable story out of her. She used to be a clarinettist, in Czechoslovakia or somewhere, and was going home after rehearsal one day when she was literally kidnapped by gangsters – right by her own front door – and taken to somewhere in the middle of nowhere where she was stuffed full of drugs and kept prisoner for weeks and raped over and over by those bastards. After a while, they gave her a red suitcase with some of her clothes and her clarinet inside. How they got hold of her clothes, who knows. And they gave her another jab and she woke up in a whorehouse somewhere in Europe, her passport stolen – and her self-respect and her future basically. And that's how she ended up in Iceland. She told Kalli all this, and he was so upset that he phoned Óli the bank manager the following day and persuaded him to pay for her release. He went back to the club and got the owner to sell him her contract and then brought her here to conduct the choir, play the church organ and teach music to the kids. He and Sidda have looked after her and protected her ever since. A great story, don't you think?'

She keeps watching the woman on the bike till she passes out of sight. She smiles dully.

'Yeah, sure. Why are you telling me this?'

'Um, I don't really know.'

'She probably slept with him, yeah?'

'No, you really think that?'

'Oh, Gunnar, you're always so naive!'

She smiles as she says this, and there is a hint of fondness in her voice; he reacts as if he's never heard anybody pay him a greater compliment. He pours her a cup of coffee and offers her a tray of Danish pastries that he bought at the bakery earlier, after she rang to say she was on her way. He pours himself a cup and now there's a new tone to his voice, no longer cheerful and impersonal but quiet and confidential: 'So, how have you been all these years?'

All these years. They went to high school in Reykjavík together, renting a room from her aunt, who lived in a three-bedroom flat in a block in Sólheimar. The aunt provided their meals and treated them as if they were her own children, always trying to get them to have their hair cut or buy new clothes, to read this or that book, watch more edifying films, do something improving. They were a bit embarrassed by all the attention, but also liked it, and for a while they almost became twelve-year-olds. Every morning they took the bus to school and sat in lessons together, and in the evenings they watched TV with the aunt, who had thoughtfully cooked them meatballs or fried fish. Sometimes she would rent films by Fellini or Bergman or Woody Allen, which they watched with her. Sometimes they retreated to his room and set up the grey acoustic panel and lay there in each other's arms, whispering about themselves and the world.

Gradually, they began to notice that the world was not some solid, undivided slab of stone standing in their way, but rather a fusion of countless ideas and experiences, of people, colours and forms in a million different nuances and hues. She would still occasionally visit him in his room with her guitar, and they would sit cross-legged facing each other and make music together, she on her electric guitar and he on his scruffy old Korean instrument that kept losing pitch, and when he tweaked it back into tune that too became part of the music. But now the lyrics were about strange women they had seen on the bus, about trees and about snowmen. At school she always wore a green parka she'd bought in a charity shop, while he went around in a black duffel coat and let his blond hair grow into ever newer and more intricate – and innocent – curls. When they started drinking, the alcohol confused and disinhibited them, they argued, trying to tear their pain off each other. They would run away into the night, somewhere out into the city, until they fell asleep, exhausted, in strange places, sometimes together, sometimes apart. The next night they would lie in each other's arms in his room once again, caressing each other and humming softly. Days passed – months, years.

One evening, the school gave a concert; they took part, she with her electric guitar and he with his battered, out-of-tune twanger, and she sang her song about how everything was going to be all right. Afterwards people crowded round, telling them how fantastic they were; from then on, they became a regular feature of such musical evenings, the song became their year's signature tune and everybody wanted to be their friend. They welcomed that and became popular because they were both sweet-tempered and fun to be with. Every summer, they went back home and worked in the fish factory to earn money, even though their parents paid her aunt for their board and lodging. These holidays always brought them closer, because they knew the world in Valeyri. They recognized all the foibles of the local weather, the lives of the people, the mountain, the valley, the sea. Sometimes they went for a drive to the head of the valley and made love there on a woollen rug the colours of the Icelandic flag; but other than that, those summer months revolved around fish. And at the end it was always a relief to get back south to the aunt, who welcomed them by roasting a leg of lamb and renting *Fanny and Alexander.*

One day he came out of a physics lesson and saw her talking to a bunch of girls, and although he was her boyfriend and they were always together, for some reason he hesitated before joining the group. When he asked her about them that evening, she said that they were just a fun crowd. The next day he saw her talking to the girls again, only now some boys had joined in. She was laughing, but when her eyes met his, hers said that this was not the right moment to join the group. They still went to the same classes, but she didn't always sit next to him, and gradually they stopped being together as much as before. Sometimes she dressed in a white blouse and wore perfume. Sometimes he sat alone with her aunt drinking tea, watching *Inspector Morse* and eating crackers with jam. Spring had arrived by the time they finally went to a party together to meet her girlfriends, and they both drank too much, became agitated and started arguing about their pain, before storming off separately, aimlessly, into the night. The girls manged to bring her back and gathered protectively around her, while he wandered around in the Reykjavík night and was once more alone in the world. He returned to the Sólheimar flat early in the morning to find that she wasn't there. Maybe she was with her friends. Maybe she wasn't. They spoke the following day and promised each other that they would never quarrel again. A promise that they kept.

They graduated that spring. He had his hair cut and let her aunt buy him a new suit, and then their parents arrived in Reykjavík to join the celebrations. His dad got drunk and disappeared for some days, so the celebrating turned into worrying. And yet on graduation day the sun shone, they both wore the traditional white student caps, and they went to have their photo taken with their arms around each other. Gunnar still has the picture, framed, here in the living room of his summer house.

After graduation, he went back home to the fish factory, while she remained in Reykjavík, where her aunt had found her a job in a shop. They spoke on the phone every evening, giving each other words that served as provisions for their journeys into loneliness. She said she loved him. She said she couldn't live without him. She said she cried herself to sleep every night. He said, 'Yes, I know. Yes, me too.' He often gazed at Svarri, the mountain that overlooks the village, thinking that the shape of it reflected some feeling in him – perhaps the feeling of being left behind. He longed to give this feeling a musical form; he felt that this form lived inside him. When he told her about it, she said, 'Yes, absolutely. I know.' He finally came to Reykjavík on Midsummer Day, and they went to a party at her girlfriends' place in the west end of town. They had too much to drink, but sat opposite each other all evening with their legs crossed and their pain between them, she with her electric guitar and the little amplifier and he with the scruffy old guitar from Korea that kept going out of tune so he was continually having to fiddle with the pegs, and she sang: *It'll all be all right – it won't go wrong / It'll all be all right – just sing this song / I told you so, I told you so.* Her friends watched and listened. He, on the other hand, had no one in the world to turn to except her. Towards morning, they wandered around the Thingholt area as if lost – which they weren't – and when they got to Amtmannsstígur it was as if they'd found the place that doesn't exist. The place where time doesn't exist. He'll remember that morning for ever.

A week later she went abroad to study, leaving him with all the words she had said to him. He remembers them all.

'I've been fine,' she says. 'I came to bury my mum. Did you know that she died?'

'Yes. I'm so sorry for you.'

'What about you?'

'I come here sometimes in the summer, to the old house, just to keep an eye on the place. It's all I have, apart from some dump in Reykjavík. How about you?'

'I got married. Got a husband. And you?'

'No, I'm on my own. I teach music. You?'

She smiles and puts down her half-eaten Danish pastry.

'Yeah, me too. D'you want to know more about me?'

'No. Yes. I don't know.'

'Why don't we go for a walk?'

'Good idea,' he says nervously.

They get up, slip into their coats, and he holds the door open for her, putting his free hand into his jacket pocket. Where he keeps his harmonica.

Now All Is Still

The evening can come now, Sidda thinks. Back at home, there's fish soup cooling slowly in an enormous pan, ready for the party; she has hoovered, washed the floors, made the beds, and everything is in its place in cupboards. And now there'll be the concert, where Kalli will sing the solo from *Night* – that slow, beautiful song that always makes her think of a bird gliding just above the sea late at night. Nobody sings it like he does. Nobody sings as smoothly as he does.

He sang it when they met for the first time, many years ago, at a dance in the Súlnasalur at Hótel Saga. Binni Frank's band was playing, and a bunch of trade unionists had turned up after a Labour Federation meeting, and were sitting round a table talking loudly, laughing and drinking vodka and ginger ale. Kalli was out on the dance floor the whole time, in his shirtsleeves, his jacket on the back of a chair somewhere, swinging the women to and fro, happily jiving, and you couldn't tell whether he was maybe married to one of them. But then he spotted her, a wallflower propping up the bar, watching the dancing, watching him, wanting to leave but not gone yet, not really knowing what she was doing there; her sister and her husband had persuaded her to come, but they'd long since left. He was in mid-jive, flushed and sweaty in his white shirt, having swung his partners to and fro, his broad back damp with sweat and his sturdy chest bursting with lust for life. He knew all the dances, new and old – pure energy and joy. He walked over to her through the din and smoky gloom, picked up a couple of tall glasses from the bar, filled them with water, and handed her one. Clinking glasses, he said, 'Cheers, sweetheart, here's to life,' and gulped down his drink.

Tonight they will dance themselves silly. Óli from the bank will play his accordion – not too quickly or he'll mess it up – Kalli says he's the only man he knows who has to have sheet music to play 'Old MacDonald Had a Farm' – Teddi will be on guitar and skipper Guðjón on snare drum, and Kata Choir will play bass guitar, the one that Kalli has somewhere in his barn, buried beneath all the junk, complete with leads and amplifier and everything. That's the full line-up of the Óli Smartypants Dance Band. They'll play anything people ask for and more, and everybody will sing and dance, Kalli louder and for longer than anybody, and the whole house will reverberate with song and happiness. The neighbours might start complaining around three o'clock, but they'll be invited to join them. And so will anyone else who'd like to come.

Sidda smiles to herself. Which is good, because Andrés is in the middle of one of his stories, and he'll be hurt if no one smiles. She has been sitting here sipping Fríða's dandelion wine, listening to that story about Halvorsen the chemist and his silly way of talking that the men here never tire of. She feels completely alone. Sometimes when she's not with Kalli she becomes aware that she isn't from round here. In spite of all these years. And there is this woman visiting Andrés and Fríða who keeps going on about a dead child she dreamed about last night or saw in the house. She's fair-haired, a bit full of figure, and there is something in her eyes that suggests that she isn't all right. It's uncomfortable. She's probably a drinker. She's bringing unrest.

And here comes Kata on her bike. She raises her hand and waves to them. Sidda waves back and shouts, 'Hi, Kata! See you later!'

Now the evening can come, with fish soup and happiness. The house will be filled with choir and merriment. They'll sing until dawn, dance and stamp their feet and be happy. She can taste the soup: fennel, white wine, garlic, tomatoes, saffron, halibut, haddock, trout – all kinds of flavours. Later, they will add the shellfish and bake the bread she's kneaded. At some point just before the concert she will catch Kalli at the fridge, eating butter with a spoon – to get the *extra richness*. As if he needed it, he, the epitome of energy and joy.

She's looking forward to the evening. And the very best bit will be the concert, when the choir hums as one, Kata plays those strong, slow, low notes of the intro on the piano, and Kalli steps forward to sing: *Now all is still within the dale…*

What she'd first noticed about him at that dance in the Súlnasalur ballroom was his arms lifted up high as he danced, the damp circles in his armpits, his puffed-out chest, his back so broad, his embrace so generous. And when he spotted her, the wallflower, he stopped dancing, his grin disappeared and he just looked at her until his face lit up in a smile. And then suddenly he was there, raising a glass of water to her and showering her with questions about herself and her parents and work and colleagues – whether she was spoken for. And yet he wore a ring. She'd noticed that straight away. He invited her to come and sit with the union guys and she accepted. He offered her a cigarette and then he offered her a vodka and tonic. She accepted it all.

And suddenly he was singing to her: *Where, O my sweetheart, say where have you been? / You know that I love you, fair maid of my dreams.*

Sidda had never been called the fair maid of someone's dreams before.

Once she's added the shellfish the soup will be perfect, and she's looking forward to dishing it out at the party and seeing the sparkle in people's eyes as the night wears on. There will be plenty of white wine and red wine and dandelion wine. Sveinsína will lend a hand, as she usually does, and Guðjón and Teddi will bring the snare drum and the guitar. Kata Choir will borrow the bass guitar from Kalli and Óli from the bank will play the accordion; they'll start the usual routine with Kata's song, of course.

They always start with that one, and everyone will join in with gusto. Some of the guests will hang about on the fringes, comparing notes about children and grand-children and maybe ancient liaisons; a couple may creep into the laundry room to let love unfold – all those village secrets. Some will stay in the kitchen listening to Andrés telling the story of Halvorsen the chemist and Lárentíus the sheriff and the funny way they spoke. But most people will go into the living room to dance and sing with the Óli Smartypants Dance Band: *She wore a siiiingle wed-ddiiing riiiiing!* They'll laugh and howl and cry, drink and dance. They will be full of passion. That's what the choir parties are always like, especially the ones here at Skjól, and they always give Sidda an intense feeling of belonging. This is where her friends and community are, in spite of everything, even though she sometimes feels completely alone when Kalli isn't with her. It's always been just the two of them.

Over the universal stillness shines the sun, dancing in the dandelion wine; a gentle gust ripples through the grass and a wagtail flits away to wherever wagtails go in the evening when they are tired. She is looking forward to the evening, the fish soup, the singing and dancing, the company, the friendship and joy. Most of all she's look-ing forward to the choir humming in unison as quietly as Kata Choir can get them to, and the sombre but gentle piano intro that she always thinks sounds like the dance of a melancholic seal, and Kalli stepping forward to sing the solo. Then all goes quiet, and the lights dim, and the song takes flight, soars like a bird gliding above the shoreline. Wearing his white shirt, Kalli raises his arms like he always does, living the song; he raises his eyebrows, embraces the audience and the whole community, his expression open-hearted as always – and then that velvet voice floats over them: *Now all is still within the dale…*

In a World of His Own

When Lalli goes about the village, he struts and darts
his eyes around like an inquisitive puffin. The villagers
are all familiar with his distinctive waddle and smile to
themselves when they see him. He isn't only called Lalli
Puffin. Kalli sometimes refers to him as 'His Absent-
Mindedness'. And here he is now, strutting as ever along
Strandgata, catching the buzz from the garden party at
the end of the street, where Andrés from the museum
and Fríða live. That is exactly where he's heading: he
needs to ask Fríða to work at the Puffin tonight, despite
having originally given her the evening off. But his head
is stuffed with umpteen thoughts, and he's gone down
one street after another, paused, looked around, turned.
It's taken him quite a while to get here. There's a staff-
ing problem, and Fríða needs to come and fill in for the
girl who was supposed to fill in for her. She vanished
into thin air, disappeared, went somewhere. Or did he
maybe forget to tell her? He can't remember. In any case,
somebody will have to take the orders and keep that chef
from down south on the straight and narrow and away

from the vermouth. He can't do that himself; he would immediately forget everything on his way to the kitchen.

He is becoming forgetful.

He has been famous for his absent-mindedness for years, and many are the funny stories about him forgetting this or that – even himself, sometimes – but lately this has become more than simple forgetfulness. He actually seems to get so distracted that he can't find the way back to himself.

They don't call him Puffin out of malice. Most people here are fond of him, so it isn't one of those nicknames, so common in small communities, intended to remind people of the worst moment of their life, never allowing them to escape from it. Lalli just happens to be a little bit like a puffin. He still has his ginger hair, even in his late seventies, and it still sticks out in all directions like a mass of raised swords because of some kind of gel he uses. He is small – he says that he is 'of almost average height' – and struts about with his chest puffed out, mouth open, cheerfully darting his eyes around. All that's missing is the stripy nose.

He is the definitive village man, but with the manners of a man of the world; a true-blue conservative who always attends Independence Party conferences, but also a staunch opponent of the quota system they introduced. He's used to people doing as he says, but very friendly; he greets everyone he meets with a jolly smile, sometimes calling them 'my dear', like a very unassuming king addressing his subjects, especially those he doesn't recognize.

He is becoming a bit forgetful.

Just at this moment, he doesn't remember why he's on his way to Fríða's. He's been strutting back and forth around the village and has come full circle. He stands and looks musingly at the village hall. He's sure that it'll come back to him as soon as he sees Fríða. She has such a positive effect on him. He's sure that everything will come back to him one fine day.

He does, however, remember the interview he did on the radio today about this evening's Valeyri Choir concert. He replays it over and over in his head. He was really good. The chirpy radio lady asked him where the name 'Valeyri' came from. He explained, as he always does when asked this question, that 'Val' has the same root as *valmenni*, the Icelandic word for a good chap, a sterling character, so 'Valeyri' simply means a sterling sandbank or spit of land, which it is indeed, a sterling place inhabited by sterling characters. That made the radio lady laugh.

He sees Kata Choir arriving on her bike at the village hall and disappearing inside with her backpack over her shoulder. He remembers it all now: he is on his way to Fríða's, to ask her to fill in at the Puffin tonight. That's it! Of course it has come back to him. There it was. There's a concert later at the village hall. That girl Kata is the conductor of the choir – Kata, the one on the bike just now. A good-looking girl. And a good name. Katrín means 'the pure one'. His mother was also called Katrín. That's how everything comes back to you, if you just stay calm. And now he remembers too that the last time he'd explained Valeyri's name Andrés from the museum had ticked him off and said that was utter nonsense, it had originally been Hvaleyri ('Whale Spit') and then the H had dropped off. But that skipper fellow – the one who's crazy about birds – married to that woman who is Kalli's sister – had protested, saying that the name came about because falcons, *valir*, had once been common here and the spit had taken its name from them. Valeyri.

Lalli thinks that actually he should be the one to decide this. He thinks that his explanation is by far the most credible, and perfect for promoting the place as a tourist destination. He once used *The Sterling Sandbank* in a brochure with a lovely picture of a puffin which he'd taken himself.

He still feels it's more or less up to him to run the place, that he's responsible for it all, even though he's no longer involved in anything apart from his shop and running the restaurant.

He tells everyone that the village was founded by his grandfather Lárus Halldórsson, who came here from the east of Iceland. But according to the local history that Andrés is writing, the community came into being during the last decades of the nineteenth century, based on fishing, trade and butchery, and Lárus Halldórsson was merely one of the many who'd settled here – although he certainly prospered, specializing in trading and providing services to farmers. And his son Lárus – Lalli Lár – who

was all things to all men well into the 1970s, is to most
people, of course, the true father of the village. He was
'the Boss'.

Lalli Puffin has never quite managed to be 'the Boss'.
He is, however, pleased with his interview with the jolly
radio lady, not least for having emphasized that there was
plenty to do here, plenty of work and plenty of people.
A community of nearly a thousand souls was damned
good – and everybody in work, all really industrious,
whether they came from Poland or Reykjavík or simply
from here. He is pleased with the way things have gone
here and feels that to an extent it's due to him.

He wanders off again, into the housing developments,
never properly planned, that just grew outwards from
the harbour, germinated like the seeds of the dandelion
clock that fall where the soil is right. Despite the lack of
planning, the area has expanded like ripples from a pebble
thrown into water. The newest houses are furthest away
from the harbour and closest to the mountain, Svarri.
Before he knows it, Lalli has arrived at the outermost
semicircle where the flat-roofs are, the ones he doesn't
think look like houses at all. In fact, nobody refers to
these boxes as houses – these blocks of flats and car repair
workshops and warehouses that seem to be saying: *Look
somewhere else, if you want to see something beautiful.
We are not houses, we are containers for activity, and
thus testimony to prudence and diligence, because the
ugly is always cheap and the cheap is always ugly, and
the more expensive something is, the more attractive it*

is, and the more attractive it is the more, much more, expensive it is. And now he suddenly finds himself at the petrol station, with the teenagers who hang out there looking up and staring at him – wary, but also open and ready to experience something new in this place where they feel like *nothing at all*. He walks gravely past their tables, past a table where an old-timer sits with a plate of deep-fried chicken nuggets and a pilsner. Lalli returns his familiar greeting with a hearty, 'Well, hello, my dear chap!' and hurries into the loo, where he sits down for a while without lowering his trousers, catching his breath before emerging and leaving with an air of having completed important business.

He turns back towards the harbour. The first two semi-circles he passes contain the villas. These belong to the people who, given their status, should really have settled in the innermost semicircle, where he lives, but regarded its prefabricated Norwegian houses as uninhabitable, rotten hovels. This is where the skippers and trades-men, foremen in the refrigeration plant, office managers, store managers and seamen live. These are the pillars of society – and their homes reflect that fact, observing the inviolable rule about the correlation between beauty, size and cost. They are concrete, two-storey buildings, with all kinds of projections and Roman arches, stand-ing gloomily on plots sporting vast green lawns centred around garden gnomes that try to look as if they belong there, with water dribbling from feeble fountains designed by experts from Reykjavík.

Lalli Puffin would probably not say this out loud to anybody, apart from Fríða at the Puffin – to whom he has said it frequently – but he is proud of himself for not having moved to higher ground, for remaining in the centre of the village. His sister, Lára Lár, on the other hand, owns the largest of the villas. After their parents, Lalli Lár and Katrín, had passed away, the siblings had split the family enterprises between them: she took over the Valeyri Fish Factory and the trawler, he took over the commercial business and the abattoir. Everything she touched thrived. In his hands, everything withered. Before long, Lára began to criticize the way her brother ran things and voiced doubts about some of his business ventures. He tolerated it all because Lára was his very own sister, five years older than him, and he had always felt that his main duty in life was to do as she said. But now they haven't spoken for at least twenty years. And they've developed a knack for not encountering each other in the village, as if they have a built-in radar that keeps them apart.

That radar is actually about to malfunction, like everything else in Lalli's life. Lára is on the point of coming round the corner and bumping into him.

The old Norwegian prefabs often feature on postcards, and people come from Reykjavík expressly to admire them and imagine for a brief moment what life in a village such as this would be like, and to visualize themselves in a village like this, and how great it would be to discover what it's like to live in a place where the most important thing that happens is that the vicar's daughter falls in love with the doctor's son and the shopkeeper's son falls in love with the barber's son. And then the tourists visit Lalli at the Puffin for a meal of cod with garlic and fennel and white wine, thinking that he is 'the Boss'.

Perhaps he is. But life itself is outside – economic life, that is: the abattoir, which the valley farmers still use, though Lalli had to sell it to pay off his debts and which is now part of a chain of abattoirs; the refrigeration plant, which is always in work because the trawler *Lárus Halldórsson VA* regularly lands its catch there; the warehouses and other buildings of the Valeyri Fish Factory. And all round the inner semicircle, side by side with the prefabs, are homes that the early settlers built themselves; the families that have grown up, lived and worked there, generation after generation, are often nicknamed after their houses (*Klumba*, *Brimnes*, *Skjól*...), or have the house names tacked onto their own like surnames. Lalli Puffin struts around looking at these houses, sometimes remembering things about them and sometimes not... You can see that the people built them themselves – some of them are comically lopsided but inspired by beautiful thoughts; others are not comical but parsimoniously beautiful; others are beautiful because of their history. Some are ugly because their lack of maintenance testifies to sloth and apathy; and some are ugly because of something that has happened there. Some of them have been renovated by the younger generation, others are derelict or have been demolished and replaced with box-like non-houses.

All these old houses have souls.

Lalli Puffin lives in the heart of the village, over the old shop which he still runs with astonishing lethargy. People go to the Bónus supermarket to do their real shopping and then pop into Lalli's out of kindness to buy an ancient stock cube or dried-out cigarettes, which he still sells singly even though that's against the law. In Lalli's hands the shop is gradually disintegrating, like all his other businesses, whether inherited from his parents or started up by himself. There is in fact hardly anything on offer there any more, apart from Lalli himself. Milk was the first to disappear from the shelves, then the vacuum-packed meat, the eggs, the bread – all the fresh produce. He still has packet soup, tinned peas, baking powder, cardamom drops, Angel Delight, KitKats in the old wrappers, Matchbox cars and shabby dolls. Kalli says that going to his shop is like going to a séance.

Lalli lives there on his own. His wife, Jakobína, died many years ago.

Next to Lalli's shop is the old village hall, with its imposing sign in old-fashioned lettering – THE VALEYRI VILLAGE HALL – in which they used to show films, stage plays directed by theatre people from Reykjavík, have meetings, concerts – and the dances. Now part of the building is occupied by the Puffin restaurant, which Fríða runs although Lalli is technically the owner. But tonight it's the venue for the Valeyri Choir's performance.

The village has its own history, its characters, its legends. The characters and legends have long since gone and all that is left are people and events. The villagers are nonetheless proud of the place, especially the ones who have moved away but flock back every summer to their forebears' quaint houses and this strange reality that lives on somewhere in their blood – the men stop shaving, put on ugly jumpers and trundle down to the harbour, hands buried deep in their pockets, while the women plait their hair and start knitting and baking, in between reading Danish fashion magazines from the 1950s that they've dug out of a cupboard.

Reverend Sæmundur sometimes says in his sermons that the village is 'beyond the world and all the perils thereof'. Smyrill the poet, on the other hand, always says in his yearly address to the Fishermen's Festival that the village is the world itself in a nutshell. Neither is true. The world is blessed with a million nuances of human life and nature that cannot be found here in Valeyri. And, as attested to by the rooftop satellite dishes, the SUVs on the streets, the graffiti on the buildings, the young people's wanderlust, the Polish migrant workers and the Asian women in the fish factory who keep the local economy going, Valeyri is immeasurably far from being 'beyond the world' or not needing it at all. The world buys the fish that is caught by the ships registered here.

And even though the revenue from fishing doesn't all end up here – who knows, maybe only a tiny part of it does – Lára Lár and latterly her son, Jói, have always taken great care to ensure that their crews include local seamen, and have kept fish processing going all year round – running at a great loss, of course, and out of pure altruism.

Lalli Puffin, on the other hand, is Valeyri's representative to the rest of the world. The tourists who flock here think that he is 'the Boss'. He actually thinks that himself.

For a long time, he did seem to be all things to all people, or at least many things to many people, because most of his enterprises turned out to be ill-judged. He started up a car dealership, a fashion boutique, a bookshop, a video-hire place and a cake shop. All came to nothing. He imported a Danish dance teacher, a Hungarian music teacher, a fly-tying expert from Hafnarfjörður and a baker from Hornafjörður. All vanished without trace.

Every morning he wakes up with the memory of Emilía in his head; he feels her hands, her deep voice, her hair, her smile, her scent, her touch, her youth – and his own youth. He has been with her all night and, half awake, he can still see her. Her hands, when she stopped salting the fish for a moment to take her gloves off and wearily rearrange her headscarf. Her eyes, as she suddenly looked up and met his gaze – eyes that were ice-blue.

That summer long ago, everything had been so blue in the light of the sun. When it rained, the drops were huge and saturated with energy. When the wind blew, it was full of promise. Every morning he woke up happy, eager to go down to the quayside to supervise the herring-salting. His father, Lalli Lár, was having an operation in Reykjavík, and his mother and sister, Lára, had gone with him; Jakobína was with her sister in Vopnafjörður. He was in charge of everything.

Sometimes Emilía would be working at the centre of the quay, sometimes at one end or the other, but he always located her and didn't let her out of his sight for the rest of the day, although he avoided looking at her directly. He strutted around trying to look authoritative but also kind; he tried to come across as a wise superior. Sometimes of an evening he saw her out walking with a coarse-looking man, presumably her husband. He discovered that his name was Sigurður and that he worked on a herring boat. Lalli longed to send Sigurður's boat to the Greenland fishing grounds, like dispatching troops to the Eastern Front, as it were. But he couldn't; apart from what Lalli Lár, his father, had ordained, it was the skippers themselves who made the decisions. Still, Lalli was drawn to Emilía, like a moon to a planet.

That summer, the herring flooded in. Everybody worked all the time, full of excitement and chatter. Nobody slept. Day and night were blindingly bright, with not a moment's silence: unending shouts and cries, music, laughing, moaning, weeping, the clattering of machines, chitchat, constant buzz and frenzy. The herring flooded in and the women could hardly keep up with the salting; the whole place teemed and after work couples would disappear into the Láfalaut hollow, which was sufficiently out of sight for them to do whatever they did undisturbed. Colours were intense, joy was palpable, tempers bubbled and surged. Lalli felt as if all of Valeyri's economy throbbed between his legs.

Those hands. She sat by herself in the village hall, with those white hands in her lap, watching people dance while an overexcited accordion player squeezed away at his instrument, half-crazy with fatigue and amphetamines. She was wearing a blue dress. He sat down next to her and asked if he could buy her a drink. She said no. He asked if he could ask her to dance. She said no. He asked if she minded if he had a small glass of something and whether he could sit by her. Silent, she looked at him with her ice-blue eyes and then turned her head away without answering, but he could see a hint of a smile at the corner of her mouth. Then they were silent.

Warmth emanated from her, and although she responded to most of his approaches with a demure 'no', she did not get up and leave; she even seemed happy for him to stay there. So he introduced himself properly and began to tell her of his interest in gardening and poetry. He paused, then stroked his sideburns and asked, 'What about you?' She said she was married, her husband was on a herring boat, his name was Sigurður and he was six foot seven inches tall and correspondingly strong. And completely lost it when drunk. He said, 'In that case, better look out,' but he had already established that the man was at sea. She watched the accordion player wheezing away at 'The Hreðavatn Waltz' while everybody whirled around the dance floor, tired and excited. She smiled listlessly. He offered her a cigarette; she accepted, inhaled the smoke with relish, then turned and blew it straight into his face.

They were silent, smoking. Kalli Skjól and his friend Gúndi came and sat next to them and began to tell stories of the old vicar and Halvorsen the chemist. Talk moved on to the fishing, new cars, tractors and haymaking in the valley. Lost in thought, Lalli sipped his schnapps and contributed the odd comment to the conversation, all the while intensely conscious of her presence next to him. Every morning when he wakes, he can feel it. Every morning he remembers that evening. Something from it always comes to him when he is half-awake – how they sat like this and their bodies engaged in still, silent conversation. And then everybody went out into the dazzling clamorous light, and they walked hand in hand along the path back to his home and she wanted to and they closed the door and kissed. Her belly naked and warm against his. Her scent like the perfume of the sea, her deep voice, those hands. The trips during the following weeks, when they drove up to the head of the valley and laid a woollen rug in the colours of the Icelandic flag on the ground and made love. Now he wanders around the streets with his mind full of Emilía and the great herring summer he spent with her – lost in thought and in her.

He is about to bump into his sister, here on the corner. They haven't spoken for years, they don't meet at social gatherings, they always find out if the other one will be there and stay away if the answer is yes.

Maybe Lára never liked him, right from the beginning, and simply put up with having to keep an eye on him in those early years. She didn't like his way of doing things. How he ran the shop, embarked on all sorts of ill-thought-out enterprises on a whim, brought in all sorts of idiots who had no place here. She saw no future in the shop, and invited him to come and join her in the fish factory and then buy into one of the big supermarkets in Reykjavík and negotiate for them to open a branch here. He ignored her completely, said he knew what he was doing, he liked doing it, it was in his blood and he had to do things his own way. When the quota system was set up, he said he didn't believe for one minute that it would last, and when she repeated her offer of a share in the Valeyri Fish Factory and tried to explain to him what a goldmine the quota system would turn out to be, he said he preferred to rely on the shop and the abattoir. Whereupon she shook her head in disapproval, her lips pinched in scorn. She was a pillar of this community, though she had very little contact with the actual villagers. There were many who had never seen her and had no idea what she looked like, and many of those she had encountered had forgotten what she looked like: mousy hair, horn-rimmed glasses, thin lips, a rather pretty face with a small chin. Despite everything, she and Lalli continued to meet and disagree. She felt responsible for looking out for her irresponsible little brother, if only for the sake of Jakobína, her one friend and the only person she could talk to about her husband, who spent every day drunk and insensible, a luckless intellectual.

He should have been a better husband. But he could have been worse too, like that man of Lára's, whatever his name was, what a boozer. Such are his daily thoughts as he reflects on the past during his circuit past this house and that, down this street and that, and then this one again and down another, so this simple huddle of houses gradually turns into the maze of his loneliness.

It wasn't that he was unkind; he always tried to meet Jakobína's wishes, all the ones he was capable of meeting. He travelled abroad with her every year, to Denmark and Italy, accompanying her everywhere. Once there, she would sit unspeaking from morning to evening, her expressionless face carefully sunscreened and turned to the sun, while he scavenged the town for stuff to sell in his shop. They made love once a month, and that was all very amicable but they never had a child. He bought her a car and a sofa and all kinds of chairs and cushions, and all the clothes, all the books and records she fancied. He paid for her evening classes, some of which he tried to set up himself, with mixed success; she enjoyed these, and made suggestions for various arts and crafts items to sell in the shop. That went well.

When she got her thrombosis, he sat with her for days, reading to her from old chronicles of the region and from the book of poems by Guðmundur, the poet of poets. As he held her hand, he felt her life draining away and knew he had to focus completely on being by her, with her – whole and undivided. Emilía and Sigurður had long since left; she lived on only in his memories, in his blood and his dreams. Knowing that Jakobína was dying, he thought that he should do one decent thing in his life, since everything else he had done had been such a failure and he had turned out to be so useless when anything depended on him. He decided he must confess his sins to his wife, unburden himself, in the hope that before she passed away they would once more become as one before God. He sat at her bedside, held her hand and told her about the summer when the herring flooded in and everyone went crazy with activity, joy and desire – he too. He described Emilía, and although he tried not to show his emotion, it got the better of him and his voice quivered with suppressed passion. He told Jakobína that Emilía had come to him once, after he had ended their relationship, with the news that their affair had borne fruit, that she was pregnant and that he now had a choice whether to live in a loveless marriage or build a family around his little child. She herself wanted to leave Sigurður because he was a bad man. But Lalli had told her to go, never to return, because he loved his wife. The herring had also gone, the sun had departed and the joy had died away. He never saw Emilía again, except in his dreams. She vanished, he said, with a gesture expressing her disappearance. When he looked up at his wife, she was no longer feeble. Nor was she stricken with grief. Her face white with fury, she hissed, 'Get out!'

Thus he lost his wife. She immediately sent for her sister-in-law, Lára, and the two of them stayed locked in the bedroom for some time, before Lára had her moved to a hospital, where she later died. He was never allowed to see her again.

She vanished, he said with a gesture.

One day there were new people living in *Brimnes*, and he never found out what had happened to Sigurður and Emilía. He thought about it every day – even expecting a visit from some young person saying: *You are my father.* But it never happened. He imagined they'd moved to America, or even Australia, as many did during those years after the herring had gone. *There's a flower that grows in Melbourne*, he sometimes sang to himself. But he couldn't be sure. They disappeared so suddenly and so utterly.

All these secrets in one village. Even where he's going now might be a secret. He can't remember at all who he was going to see. Was he going to see Kalli Skjól and borrow a bit of chicken wire from him, to stick in that gutter where the starlings are making themselves far too much at home…? Or was he maybe on his way to see Fríða? Yes – that was it, wasn't it? Wasn't he about to ask Fríða to cut his hair? Where would he be without Fríða?

He is becoming a bit forgetful.

There is so much he cannot remember. He forgets straight away whether he is going this way or that, wants to have a word with this person or that, but every morning when he is still only half-awake he remembers Emilía, what she was like and the times they had together – and then immediately remembers that he is a useless good-for-nothing. He knows she is dead. His dreams tell him that. Nothing in his life has been a success. Everything has faded and withered in his hands.

Deep in thought, he turns a corner, not noticing until it's too late that he is about to bump into a woman walking towards him. He looks at her kindly. She has white hair, horn-rimmed glasses, thin lips, a rather pretty face with a small chin, and she stares at him, panic-stricken. His face lights up in a broad smile, and he opens his arms towards her and says, 'Oh, I'm so sorry, my dear, how stupid of me, what was I thinking?'

...and Slides along the Spit

I was in a forest, following a footpath marked out by white stones. I realized that I was on some kind of a journey, that a destination awaited me, though I knew not where, when or how. Part of me understood, however, that I wasn't actually in this forest, that it was only my mind that was there. In reality, I lay in a bed in the Vífilsstaðir TB clinic. I was delirious – I was already at my journey's end. The same part of me knew that Katrín was sitting beside me, reading, knitting or holding my hand, as she had done ever since my sickness had returned some months before. She had moved south as soon as I fell ill, rented a room in Reykjavík with her mother, and came out here every day to be with me, to support me, her poet, her poet of poets.

I lay on my own. Motes of dust speckled the rays of sunlight that shone through the window. A little angel sat on the windowsill bathed in light, silent and sad, dangling his slender legs. Then I found myself in the forest again, following a footpath marked out by white stones. Now and then thick branches brushed against me, heavy with rain. I walked for ever. It was dark. From time to time I would come to a bright clearing, but there was nothing there. And I knew that I wasn't there, but here.

Katrín sat by my bed, occasionally reading to me from old Valeyri chronicles, or from anthologies by my favourite poets, Jónas Hallgrímsson, Steingrímur Thorsteinsson and Matthías Jochumsson, or poems by my friends – but never my poems, which I had asked her not to read. She didn't see my poems until long afterwards. Sometimes I wrote a poem after she left, if I was conscious and felt up to it. I wrote in a brown notebook that I kept under my pillow. I wrote things like *Life is the path that leads to death*. Inspired by nightmares, my poems were about ogres in dark ravines and young girls who encounter them and come to harm. They were about Katrín.

Often, my friend Lalli came and sat with me and talked about his pet subjects: haymaking, fishing and other such things. This cheered me.

Again I was in a forest, following a footpath marked out by white stones. It seemed to have rained recently. I thrust the sodden branches aside. I saw the path winding its way further into the darkness. I walked on. I knew I wasn't really in the forest, it was just my mind that was there, I was dreaming, I was drowsing – and yet not. My conscious self was awake, and I saw that Katrín wasn't in her usual place by my bed, that the chair was empty and had been so for some time, for several weeks. The sun's rays shone in through the window. I saw motes of dust. An angel dangled his legs from the windowsill and gazed at me with sadness. I closed my eyes and disappeared once more into the heart of the forest. I came to a bright clearing where a grey horse stood. I approached it slowly, gently, talked soothingly to it; I felt that it would guide me to my journey's end, but it started in alarm the moment I reached it and made off into the trees. I followed, eventually reaching a thundering waterfall. From the darkest depths I heard moaning. I sat on a rock, exhausted, felt the mist from the falls on my cheek, looked into the whirlpool, stroked the rock's covering of lichen, felt its roughness. I stood up and moved on. I walked barefoot across scree towards a mountainside. Everything was so bright.

I opened my eyes. I lay in the Vífilsstaðir TB clinic, alone in the ward, nothing but absence in my embrace. My conscious self was awake and I knew that Katrín's usual chair had been empty for some time. My friend Lalli came from time to time and chatted about his pet subjects, haymaking, fishing and other such things, and as he was leaving he told me that Katrín wouldn't be coming any more. She was no longer my girl. Who, then, would guide me through this dark forest of my mind? Who would stroke my hair, support me in my suffering and care for me, her poet of poets? I shut my eyes and found myself once more in a forest, following a footpath marked out by white stones. I thrust the sodden branches aside. Twigs crackled under my feet and I knew my conscious self was awake, that I was conscious, that I was on a journey – that some kind of journey's end soon awaited me, because life is the path that leads to death.

I had seen into Katrín's soul. When I had been haymaking during those long summer days in the valley back home, when I climbed Mount Svarri and looked out over the spit and into the valley trying to make a decision, when I was in a cramped cubbyhole in Reykjavík studying Latin, half-starving, and when I had tossed and turned in bed at night, planning my life – and now as I walked along this path with these twigs crackling under my feet – the sparkle in her eyes was always with me.

I walked on, out of the forest, until I reached an opening, a grey rock. I felt the wind in my hair and on my cheeks, the white sun flowed between my palms – ahead of me the ocean, as smooth as glass and deep blue – I opened my eyes and saw motes of dust, and Katrín's chair, empty for months. The little angel was gone from the white-painted windowsill. I closed my eyes and looked around this cold, grey rock. I was out in the open. I opened my eyes again and saw that the little angel was standing at my bedside, gazing at me with compassion. I wanted to confess my sins to him, but during my short life I had travelled but infrequently, had met few people, not thought a lot, not achieved much. My life had taken place in the written word and in thoughts. I was merely a consciousness. I closed my eyes but still saw the angel. He was completely white and on his forehead was a tiny horn that I hadn't noticed before. He beckoned for me to follow him. I rose from my bed and we walked together, out through the window, into the mist.

I walked along a shore, along the water's edge, barefoot, feeling the rocks cut into the soles of my feet and the cold sea caress my toes. The sky above me was silent. All was white, and in my chest I felt a heavy throbbing; from some gentle vastness came a sign that, as for me, my days were as grass. Before me stood a grey horse. I passed through a gate on the shore and the horse entered the water as I turned inland. I was on a street. Rain was falling. Mist descended and enshrouded me in grey, and I saw Katrín cross the road, here in Valeyri, and head towards the shop, entering it. She reappeared with Lalli, and I watched as they crossed the street, leading two smartly dressed children, a boy and a girl, by the hand.

I was shrouded in grey. I was pure consciousness. Katrín was lost to me for ever – who, then, would be my guide along the narrow path that led across the scrabbles of rock, across boulders, gravel, scree, abyss, through howling wind, water, blizzard and brash ice, to the final gateway?

The mist. It comes in off the sea and slides along the spit.

Subscribe

Discover the best of contemporary European literature: subscribe to Peirene Press and receive a world-class novella from us three times a year, direct to your door. The books are sent out six weeks before they are available in bookshops and online.

Your subscription will allow us to plan ahead with confidence and help us to continue to introduce English readers to the joy of new foreign literature for many years to come.

> *'A class act.'* GUARDIAN

> *'Two-hour books to be devoured in a single sitting: literary cinema for those fatigued by film.'*
>
> TIMES LITERARY SUPPLEMENT

A one year subscription costs £35 (3 books, free p&p for UK)

Please sign up via our online shop at www.peirenepress.com/shop

BASMEH & ZEITOONEH
RELIEF & DEVELOPMENT

Peirene is proud to support Basmeh & Zeitooneh.

Basmeh & Zeitooneh (The Smile & The Olive) is a Lebanese-registered NGO. It was established in 2012 in response to the Syrian refugee crisis. B&Z aims to create opportunities for refugees to move beyond being victims of conflict and help them to become empowered individuals who one day will return to their own country to rebuild their society. Today the organization is managing nine community centres in the region: seven in Lebanon and two in Turkey.

Peirene will donate 50p from the sale of this book to the charity. Thank you for buying this book.

www.basmeh-zeitooneh.org